Faces

Faces

Mohamed Choukri

Translated from Arabic by Jonas Elbousty
Foreword by Roger Allen

Georgetown University Press / Washington, DC

We are grateful for the support of this publication by the Council on Middle East Studies at the Yale MacMillan Center.

Library of Congress Cataloging-in-Publication Data

Names: Shukrī, Muḥammad, 1935-2003, author. | Elbousty, Jonas, translator. | Allen, Roger, 1942- writer of foreword.
Title: Faces / Mohamed Choukri ; translated from Arabic by Jonas Elbousty ; foreword by Roger Allen.
Other titles: Wujūh. English
Description: Washington, DC : Georgetown University Press, 2024.
Identifiers: LCCN 2023052704 (print) | LCCN 2023052705 (ebook) | ISBN 9781647124779 (paperback) | ISBN 9781647124786 (ebook)
Subjects: LCSH: Shukrī, Muḥammad, 1935-2003—Fiction. | LCGFT: Autobiographical fiction. | Novels.
Classification: LCC PJ7818.H6 W8513 2024 (print) | LCC PJ7818.H6 (ebook)
LC record available at https://lccn.loc.gov/2023052704
LC ebook record available at https://lccn.loc.gov/2023052705

∞ This paper meets the requirements of ANSI/NISO Z39.48-1992 (Permanence of Paper).

25 24   9 8 7 6 5 4 3 2 First printing
Printed in the United States of America

Cover design by Martyn Schmoll
Interior design by Paul Hotvedt

For Hicham Elbousty

And in memory of Moulay Elkebir Elbousty and Nadia Boufrouri

Contents

Acknowledgments

Twenty years have passed since the death of the Moroccan author Mohamed Choukri. *Faces* is the third novel in his autobiographical trilogy, through which he gives us a closer look at the lives and struggles of ordinary Moroccans. In bringing this work to English readers, I have relied on the generosity of amazing individuals. I am indebted to Afaf Elbousty, Karima Belghiti, Karl Otto, and Roger Allen, each of whom read the entire manuscript multiple times and offered excellent advice at different stages of the project. Roger Allen is always ready to chat about the art and problematics of translation, and I'm a direct beneficiary of his expertise and wisdom. I'm extremely thankful that he agreed to write the foreword. I'd also like to thank the anonymous reviewers for their excellent feedback and enthusiasm about this work.

It has been a great pleasure to work with Hope LeGro, and I'm indebted to her for her guidance and assistance throughout this project. Her utmost professionalism and prompt communication made this process very smooth. I'm very fortunate to have been able to work with her. I'd also like to thank Tarek Choukri, the author's nephew, who has granted me permission to translate this novel and has been generous with his time, responding to my many queries. Finally, I'd like to thank the Council on Middle East Studies at the Yale MacMillan Center for its financial support.

Foreword

Faces introduces readers of English to a relatively late example of the narrative artistry and voice of the Moroccan writer Mohamed Choukri (1935–2003). Published in 1996, it constitutes the third volume of what he has termed his "novelistic autobiography" (in Arabic, *sīra dhātiyya riwā'iyya*). Of the three volumes, it is certainly the first that is best known and indeed not a little notorious. Originally published in English in 1973, *For Bread Alone* is a rendering by the American author and composer Paul Bowles, a longtime resident of Tangier, of what is alleged to have been the first oral performance of the narrative by then-illiterate Choukri. The Arabic text, *Al-Khubz al-ḥāfī*, was not to appear in print until 1982, and Choukri himself proceeded to challenge Bowles's account of the circumstances under which the work had been conceived and performed. Choukri's narration of his childhood provides a stark and often brutal account—involving violence, prostitution, and smuggling—of Tangier's street life. He recounts that time in graphic and sometimes prurient detail, which has led several Arabic-speaking countries to ban the work—a surefire way, one might suggest, of enhancing its reputation and popularity, as

Joyce's *Ulysses* and D. H. Lawrence's *Lady Chatterley's Lover* clearly illustrate. "How will I ever be able to confront what I went through as a child?" the narrator of *Faces* asks himself in "My Face through the Seasons."

The second volume in the trilogy was published in 1992, under two different titles—*Zaman al-akhṭāʾ* (Time of errors) and *Al-Shuṭṭār* (The crafty ones). An English version appeared in 1996 as *Streetwise*, a shrewd rendering of the second title and an apt reflection of the work's contents. The illiterate narrator depicted in the first volume is now learning to read and is anxious to acquire as much knowledge as possible. At the same time, he continues the reckless conduct that marked his earlier years and led to his imprisonment. The divided existence of the narrator—part student, part debauchee—reflects a transitional phase in the life and career of a young man who has had to overcome the most terrible obstacles imposed on him by his family and society.

Faces, the third volume in the trilogy, reflects the life and career that emerged from and was transformed by those earlier experiences and escapades. The setting and social norms of Tangier are unchanged, but the narrative voice that depicts the city's people and places now takes a more detached perspective. The format of the work, divided into relatively brief segments, lends it some of the stylistic and structural features of shorter narrative genres. It is no surprise that those same traits are also found in Choukri's two collections of short stories, *Majnūn al-ward* (Flower crazy, 1979) and *Al-Khayma* (The tent, 1985)—published in English as a single volume titled *Tales of Tangier* (2023).

In *Faces,* Tangier remains in many ways what it has always been—an urban space of transit, of intercontinental contacts, of intrigue and sexual exploitation, and of social extremes exploited by some to personal gain and suffered by many others, especially women ("Tangerines"); a site that manages to attract to its streets, cafés, bars, stores, brothels, and dwellings the indigent from other parts of Morocco and beyond. In "Love and Curses," however, the first-person narrator reflects on the passage of time and his own changed circumstances when he describes the current state of the city in almost nostalgic terms: "Even the night in Tangier, which—until the very recent past— had preserved some of its youthful and beautiful spirit, has now become old, flabby, ugly, and soaked in shit." The narrator selects particularly significant locations throughout the work, providing examples of the ways in which social divides have long affected the lives of the city's residents.

It is in this changed and changing social and economic environment that Choukri introduces his readers to the figure of Fatima—or Fati, as she is usually called—a young prostitute who, following a familiar pattern, has come to Tangier from her hometown of Larache to eke out a living. She discusses the distorted dimensions of love, lust, and prostitution with a disarming candor. She is an important figure in the narrative, but so too are the author's other friends and acquaintances—each of whom contribute to the various segments of the novel and to the multiple "faces" of its title.

Choukri describes his relationship with Fati and to the lives and favorite venues of Tangier's struggling citizens in the autobiographical first person. That noted, his focus on the travails

and travels of Fati (to Denmark and Spain) and on the lives of
the city's other characters fictionalizes the narrative and situ-
ates it on the generic spectrum identified by Hayden White in
Tropics of Discourse (1978)—one that moves from history, via
biography and autobiography, to fiction. I would also suggest
that Choukri's more detached—and even reflective—narrative
voice in this third volume recalls the issues associated with
the uses and possible interpretations of the first person. The
renowned Argentinian author and critic Jorge Luis Borges il-
lustrates its potential ambiguity well in his short essay "Borges
and I," translated by James E. Irby in *Labyrinths* (New York:
New Directions, 1964): "The other one, the one called Borges,
is the one things happen to. . . . I live, let myself go on living, so
that Borges may contrive his literature, and this literature justi-
fies me. . . . Little by little, I am giving over everything to him,
though I am quite aware of his perverse custom of falsifying
and magnifying things" (246). Like its two predecessors in this
trilogy, Choukri's *Faces* is indeed best described as a novelistic
autobiography.

—Roger Allen, translator and Sascha Jane Patterson Harvie
Professor Emeritus of Social Thought and Comparative Ethics
and professor of Arabic and comparative literature at the
University of Pennsylvania

Love and Curses

Books are not made to be believed, but to be subjected to inquiry. When we consider a book, we mustn't ask ourselves what it says but what it means, a precept that the commentators of the holy books had very clearly in mind.

—Umberto Eco, *The Name of the Rose*

When experience becomes stronger than regret, feelings of guilt dissipate. I won't try through this experience to either absolve or condemn myself or others. Like a silkworm, I swing between absolute joy and absolute sorrow. Oh, if only you knew the beautiful things I wish for you and myself! What I wish for myself may even be less beautiful than what I wish for all those who share my curse. I'll never be afraid of a cursed and gloomy tomorrow—whether I'm alone or with the devil.

Even the night in Tangier, which—until the very recent past—had preserved some of its youthful and beautiful spirit, has now become old, flabby, ugly, and soaked in shit. It has turned brutal, no longer inspiring comfort or security. I'm aware that it manages to evade the charges leveled at it despite all the suspicious things that take place in it. Even though I know that night has become the godfather and accomplice of crime, I'll

1

never stand against it, turn away from it, or forget how it used to keep me company. I'm indebted to it, for it was my ally through difficult and strange times. I will not deny its beneficial side, but neither will I be complicit in its horrific crimes, which lead to the deaths of innocent people and for which it has been unwilling to repent.

The Granada Pub was never packed with patrons until Fati started working there as a bartender. The clients who used to frequent this and other seedy pubs in Tangier had never been served so delicately and flirtatiously by a beautiful blond woman who could cite, during conversations with illiterate customers, both classical and modern Arabic verse in a soft, melodious voice.

"We've got our babes back. Long live your mother, Fati!" yelled a boisterous drunkard infatuated with her.

Other escorts, bartenders, and prostitutes told vulgar and made-up stories when they spoke about their past, which was always fraught with deprivation and abandonment, and gossiped about the lives of their customers. By contrast, Fati's rich and flirty chatter drew inspiration from the books she read voraciously. Although she didn't understand much of their content, her ambition to grow and improve herself encouraged her to read every day. The only information that nosy people in Tangier could dig up on her was that she came from the city of Larache. Still, people gossiped about women like her, spreading silly rumors.

Fati left high school in her senior year and moved to this paradise, where all that remains is an illusion—the past. She came to work in the Granada Pub. That was her destiny. She was barely twenty years old.

"I never learned how to love," she used to say, "and I don't think I ever will."

I couldn't tell whether she was sincere or simply arrogant, but it didn't matter. What I could conclude from her statement was that she only understood the meaning of love through the books she read. Love did not have a place in her life; she thought about it, but she didn't experience it. Even now, she only toys with it to keep her job at the pub. She doesn't let it toy with her. We once discussed what it means to be a whore.

"I sell sex because I refuse to sell love," she replied. "This gives my life some meaning. I can sell my body to someone I don't desire, but I can also give it away out of lust. Do you know what?"

"Tell me."

"I'm not capable of thinking about real love yet." She paused for a moment, then continued, "What I mean is that love can't be sold to bastards."

What I understood from Fati was that the dreams of wealthy people are not all that different from the dreams of those who live in poverty. The same goes for their sorrows and joys.

Fati, who can be a cunning flirt when necessary, is the pub's cashier and top bartender. She always knows what to say and do. I've learned from her that many pimps and maniacs—witnesses, rich or poor, to the emptiness of human life—have wailed at her feet in moments of silliness or weakness. She finds consolation in watching those sons of bitches weep in front of her—*her*, the whore. She stays silent, pretending to listen with great interest as they go on and on with their idiotic and vulgar stories, all in the belief that they're truly important. She uses her cleverness and flirtatious games to attract customers and drive them crazy. No other woman in the pub can compete. But these moments of triumph are matched by moments of contempt. There are times when she is so afraid of her customers that her mouth dries up and she has trouble swallowing, as if confronted by a gorilla drowning his sorrows after a rough day. His eyes flicker with vicious anger as he demands to do with her as he pleases, or else he'll punch or slice open her face. He threatens anyone who tries to interfere with a fate worse than hers, maybe even death itself. What would she be with scars on her face?

You may be wondering, Did she really see that or was it all a dream? Was she only narrating what she heard?

I ask myself, Can an adventure be real if it doesn't involve a thief and a prostitute, a vagabond and a crazy woman?

It's as if heroic love can only be achieved when it's cursed—when a wealthy man falls in love with a poor girl, or a believer with an atheist. Everything is possible. People who know what true love means have taught me that love has no rules. You need to recall every happy memory or use your damned imagination. I feel sorry for people who write but cannot use their imagination. Every seductive piece of writing has a secret that makes us either admire or ignore it.

When we come across bastards who don't let us grow naturally, who are so envious of us that they steal our childhood, our youth, and our lives, our imagination becomes the only way to console ourselves and overcome the trying times that wear us down at every turn.

I remember a young man who started writing fervently, thinking that it would be his salvation. Well, according to what we've been told, writing can only be a blessing to those who are faithful to it, not to opportunists. At the time, only the smell of bitter almond blossoms would emanate from this region. That young man could not withstand the test of writing, which is merciless. No amount of mediation or bribe money could help him. The man's distressed marriage poisoned him and gave him an ulcer. He lost hope in the struggle, then gave up and suffocated. I remember that God wasn't by his side. Unfortunately for him, the woman he was madly in love with punished him. She betrayed him over and over with people he thought were his friends. Only when he passed away did she finally belong to him; she started mentioning him everywhere until she went mad. She began living between the insane asylum and the streets because she hated living under her family's roof.

I'm so lucky to have never loved such a cursed woman. She would have vanquished me. In my life there's neither vanquisher nor vanquished. I have loved women from afar, but I didn't care if they loved me back. Whenever women start to reciprocate and get serious about a relationship, disaster strikes. I want to love them from afar, and I want them to love me from afar. I want a sense of longing between us, a longing that could ignite love—if love is in the air. I don't want to love a woman that I worship in the evening and curse in the morning, as many men do. That tale is as old as time, but every explanation fails to give it its proper value. It has united us in disagreement and persevered even more than our delusions about existence have. I still struggle with loving myself, with subduing my vicious and stupid obsessions and heading toward nirvana, not karma—upward, not downward.

Can the most beautiful things be, as André Gide says, "those that madness prompts and reason writes"? Nietzsche disagrees in an aristocratic way, telling us that "the highest intelligence and the warmest heart cannot coexist in one person."

On this Tangier trip—most of which took place at night, not during the day—I obliterated a part of myself through imaginings and wanderings, hallucinations and ecstatic masturbations, memories and telepathic communications, all the while looking at whatever Zafzaf's ceiling offered for inspiration. In such a maze, who on earth would envy me and my wild obsessions?

Human filth is not confined to the toilet, unless the person is physically or mentally ill—or both—and that isn't natural. Human beings must fart, burp, yawn, sleep, live, and die.

The night isn't always sacred. It is meditation that kept Nietzsche awake, compelling him to cut his fingers with a razor blade or burn them with a candle just to confront his anxiety and pain. It is delirium that exhausted Lautréamont after he drank twenty cups of strong coffee and nobody could stop his roaming the streets of Paris. And it is human madness that abruptly ended van Gogh's life and that sent Antonin Artaud, Strindberg, and Nijinsky into seclusion. . . . Night is either pure or profane, a dream or a nightmare, devoted to peace or devoted to crime. Night takes pity on no one. You need to take pity on yourself, to make a choice and know what you want from it. For my part, I've decided to ravish my nightly feast before my desire dissipates and before I get heartburn, throw up my bile, and die.

"Fatim!"

Fatim or Fateem—this is what I called her to distinguish myself from the other men.

She perked up and shouted back, "Over here!"

"Give me a glass for free."

"Sure."

"My pockets are full of holes tonight."

"No worries. I'll mend them for you as usual, waiting for what your tomorrow will bring."

"Thanks, Penelope."

"What are you rambling on about?"

"I'm leaving with the rest of the bastards."

"Are you going to write about the children who sniff glue? These days they're like locusts invading the city at night."

"Maybe, but I'll also be writing out of a love for words, a love for the cursed journeys of words and bodies. The body is Tangier's great feast. Celebrating it should come first and last. It's offered to us on a plate, in the light of the morning sun or of the evening moon. I remember the old alleys and how, in one or another, we used to hear Jews singing the psalms of David. The sound of Jewish weddings would echo across the rooftops in the morning."

"My mom wants to get to know you. I told her all about your madness."

Lalla Chafika adopted Fati by accident. Her mother, Nezha, got pregnant with her—also by accident—when she was working as a prostitute at one of Larache's last brothels, before it was shut down after independence. Lalla Chafika was a well-respected pimp and had been since her own glorious slutty days came to an end. Even today, if she's in the mood with one of her admirers, she can still be lovely, sweet, and charming.

Nezha went over to Lalla Chafika's place and put her four- or five-year-old daughter, Fatima Zohra, in the woman's lap.

"I'm just going to visit my sister in Ceuta, and then I'll come straight back," she told Lalla Chafika, handing her a meager amount of money.

Nezha, however, never came back. She fell in love with a Spanish soldier from the tercio. When he found out that she was cheating on him with some Moroccan guy, he stabbed her with a knife. Lalla Chafika did not adopt only Fati; she adopted Yasmina and Leila, who were also left on her lap, too. She thought she'd make some money fostering the kids, but they ended up abandoned and she ended up adopting them. She had to work hard to support them. She knew that their mothers had left for other cities in Morocco or overseas and that, even if they returned to reclaim their kids, she'd never be paid for taking care of them. One boy, whose mother did come back to take him with her, cried over leaving Lalla Chafika. The mother didn't cough up a single dime, because she was even more broke than Lalla Chafika.

Maybe it was for the best that Lalla Chafika, following the advice of a woman with experience taking children in, adopted more girls than boys. She knew that the girls were usually more grateful than the boys. But both can be grateful or ungrateful.

Lalla Chafika had to put up with men's saliva, obscenity, and aggression with what was left of her youthful body, until

Fati matured and entered the domain against Lalla Chafika's will. Today Lalla Chafika doesn't whine about or regret what happened. Yasmina and Leila stayed in school and had a tough time with their studies. They began to think of Fati as their older sister or aunt. Lalla Chafika was getting tired of her jobs in small restaurants and cheap hotels. She also worked as a maid. She'd spend an hour or two here and there cleaning the houses of single men and retired widowers, who were either incapacitated by disease or fighting for their last breath. Sometimes she'd surrender to a client and have sex with him after finishing her chores. If she got double the usual pay, she'd thank God many times over and feel grateful. But if the client was a miser and a son of a bitch, she'd curse him and the day he was born. There were also clients who forced her, without any pity, into humiliating sex acts. Those sinful men never paid her a cent.

Fati's body developed enough that she could face the evil of those who thronged her. Her beauty was a fortune that every miserable girl in her position envied. She did not consider it a disgrace but her destiny and the destiny of her family. She used to believe that good things could come out of a bad situation. She promised herself that her body would replace that of Lalla Chafika, that she would use it to take care of her unfortunate family without complaint, agony, or regret. It was this that made me realize why she was reluctant to fall in love: love might've fooled her into marrying one of those bastards.

Couscous—the one dish that I hate. I had it with sheep guts the day my uncle died. I was seven years old and could barely chew it. It disgusted me. That was during the famine in the

Rif. Lalla Chafika makes it the Marrakech way—with whole
wheat, meat, and veggies. I ended up having some at her place
the day Fati introduced me. It tasted so good, so unlike the regular couscous that I had had a few times before and that I had
eaten to avoid embarrassing the kind hosts who had invited me
to their stupid family celebrations. I'm sure that Lalla Chafika
made it with secret magic and a blessing. She served it on a
tayfour platter and arranged for us to sit and serve ourselves in
a specific order. She was still a very capable seducer; her moves
were smooth and agile even though she was in her fifties. She
never forgot to put on traditional makeup and always exuded a
refinement acquired only from rich experience. She knew how
to rejuvenate what was aging her. You would've loved her—
and Fati—just as I do.

It was a school holiday. Lalla Chafika made a sneaky signal
to Yasmina and Leila after lunch, and they timidly retreated to
the other room. They were almost the same age, about fifteen,
and seemed to get along with each other, as if they had been
nursed from the same breast. They didn't look like sad orphans.
Their chests had filled out, and they must have started fondling
them.

Lalla Chafika spoiled Fati with whatever she wanted. Every
naughty girl must want a mother like Lalla Chafika. She blessed
Fati many times over the course of our lunch. She blessed me,
as Fati's friend, many times too. She blessed me because I gave
Fati all my books and companionship without expecting sex in
return. We used to flirt a lot in conversation, but deep down, I
was repressing a mysterious love for her.

Fati used to wear an embroidered purple silk bandana on her forehead, a long gray skirt, and a white blouse. She was always stuck between four walls and two things: reading in a grim house or making up stories and listening to those of some poor guys in a bar. She told me that she wanted to smell the sea, let her hair wave in its breeze, and gaze at its horizon, so I took her to the beach at the end of autumn.

"Have you ever traveled outside Morocco?" she asked.

"I visited my aunt in Melilla in 1951, on my way from Oran to Tetouan. I've never gone farther than Ceuta."

"If I weren't responsible for my family, I'd travel to the other side to see what living there is like. I might be tempted to stay and never come back."

"I thought about emigrating too, in the early sixties, but I decided to stay and see what would happen."

"You don't regret it?"

"I don't know what regret is, just as you don't know what love is."

We were walking by the edge of the sea with our shoes in our hands. The waves were splashing us, the spume washing our feet. No one was close enough to watch us. Seagulls were chirping, jumping, flying, landing on the sand, and brooding on the water. We alternated between sitting near the water's edge and walking. She had the Arabic translation of Émile Zola's *L'Assommoir* with her, and I had a *petaca*. I was gulping down Spanish cognac while she was smoking her cigarettes. We didn't care what was halal and what was haram. Dark clouds and a cold breeze buffeted our faces. She had finished the novel and was returning it to me. She didn't want her life to end like Gervaise's. I explained that we should never embody the lives of the protagonists we read about. That's what Jean Genet taught me when I told him how affected I was by the life of Julien Sorel. The fates of our characters are not necessarily our own.

"And what if their lives resemble the lives of real people?"

"It doesn't matter. Readers who emulate them, who fall under their spell, might plunge into a hellish abyss from which there's no return. There are people who have committed suicide after reading *The Sorrows of Young Werther* by Goethe, *Camille* by Dumas, or *The Stranger* by Camus."

I wasn't ashamed to walk with Fati on the streets. She wasn't the type to show cleavage, sway her hips from side to side, or put on tight pants so as to suggest "Here I am; follow me if I drive you wild." Fati's acute sensitivity stopped her from throwing herself at anyone.

We were drinking and smoking as we pleased. Lalla Chafika was in a state of utmost euphoria and radiance. Fati seemed relaxed and delighted, smoking and drinking with a sophisticated charm. She doesn't hold the smoke in her lungs for very long, unlike every damned stressed-out girl, nor does she wait until she reaches the butt to drag the cigarette slowly across the ashtray as though drawing her name in the sand. Even Lalla Chafika, who smokes her cheap cigarettes heavily, doesn't hold the smoke for very long. Any hapless girl would want a family like Fati's.

In Lalla Chafika's eyes, Fati was now the head of the household and its bread winner. If Fati's mother were to try to take her back, I think Lalla Chafika would refuse.

Lalla Chafika always has a bottle of wine. She doesn't ask
for more, but she won't abstain if more is available. If a generous man were to offer her a bottle—or more—of the kind she
likes, she'd pray for all the pious worshippers of God to bestow
their blessings upon him and grant him a prosperous life. She's
just like a soldier, in need of daily provisions no matter how
tough the times. What breaks her heart, she used to say with
a sigh, is that she rarely finds people with whom she enjoys
having a drink and indulging in pleasant conversation in the
moonlight. Whenever Lalla Chafika's longing stirred, Fati felt
sorry for her and tried to console her with memories of the past.
Fati knew how to choose a suitable client for Lalla Chafika. He
would be more or less the same age as her, generous, pleasant
while drinking, flirty, and naughty in bed. Lalla Chafika would
be satisfied with them both and bless her night with the man.

Fati made sure not to drink too much during the day because she knew she'd have work awaiting her at the bar in the
evening. She was in charge there and made good money. Her
boss was satisfied with her integrity and skill. If some damned
client, dissolute and stubborn, insisted on getting her drunk for
pleasure or with malicious intent, she'd know how to surrepti-
tiously pour the drink into the sink under the bar. And if one of
those arrogant men emptied his pockets so completely that he
couldn't afford a taxi, she'd rejoice. "Thank God," she'd say,
"that I'm not the wife of a guy like that."

She saw the way drunk girls would start behaving badly in the
arms of sly men. Those men liked seeing women in that state;
it drove them wild. You should see one for yourself, all flabby
like a tissue or sponge. She'd look hideous even if she were

beautiful. One rainy morning, I spotted one such girl crawling on the sidewalk along the main boulevard. When she couldn't drag herself any farther, she sat down on a store's doorstep. The rain was pouring. She was crying and begging for help. An older taxi driver eventually rescued her, cursing the onlookers who scoffed and did nothing to help. People can be merciless. Some of those men went on their way, asking God to protect them from the accursed devil, while others stuck around, venting their anger on fallen women.

A guy passed by with an umbrella. He was using it as a cane, moving it in rhythm with his lengthy footsteps as the rain poured down on him. I didn't pay him or his umbrella any more attention and started to leave. Then someone stopped me and asked what had happened to the woman who was no longer there. Three or four people were still at the scene: some felt sorry for the woman; others continued to curse her.

I told Fati what I had seen. She said that she has seen girls so drunk that they couldn't feel their own urine and shit dropping to their feet as they stood at the bar. Fati is scared that something like that might happen to her. That's why she's so careful, using that little trick of hers, to avoid getting wasted. She's a beautiful and attractive woman who can make any man—greedy, silly, or sane—suffer. For her part, she never suffers for anybody. There's no doubt that she learned that lesson from Lalla Chafika's painful experience with violent, perverted, and crazy men.

Fati starts work at eight in the evening, and her shift usually lasts until four or five in the morning. If she doesn't go back home, Lalla Chafika understands that she has slept with a generous gentleman. She doesn't worry about her. She has taught her how to gracefully get out of anything she doesn't want to do, how to play along with a guy until she can leave in peace, and how to avoid humiliation. She's also always armed with her miraculous amulet, which she believes protects her. Fati doesn't care so much about the age of her client as about the amount he's willing to pay. Something you need to know about her, however, is that she'll never sleep with a client whose body is not clean and whose appearance is not neat, even if he's prepared to fork up a lot of money.

Once when I was drunk, I asked her to sleep with me. I was clean and had enough money, but she rejected me kindly.

"I don't want to lose you as a friend," she said.

It was that gentle stab that made me start to resent her. How could she turn me down when she keeps sleeping with people inferior to me? I convinced myself after a while that I was wrong and naive to ask her. I also convinced myself that she wanted me but just didn't know *how* she wanted me. She was lost and had no idea what she wanted or didn't want. She was in a turmoil that she knew how to keep to herself.

Needless to say, all this happened before I met Lalla Chafika. She encouraged our friendship, which made me repress my lustful desire for Fati. Fati didn't want me to feel defeated or to spend the night masturbating, so she chose a newbie for me. The girl was as charming as Rambo on his first trip to Paris. It felt like Fati was trying to satisfy my lust for her through that girl, whom she asked to treat me as if I were her brother.

The newbie had just started coming to the bar a few days before. Fati pitied newbies just as much as she hated the sneaky professional girls who were always eager to take revenge on decent guys, even if they had no reason. If she found out that you were fooling around with or abusing those self-absorbed newbies, she'd get angry.

"Damn," I thought to myself. "Does she want to go on an adventure with me, the likes of which you read about in the courtly love poetry I've mostly forgotten?"

That's her game, but she needs to play it with somebody else. I had my own game, one that I used to seduce and trick whomever I wanted. That's what I used to say to protect myself and overcome my lust for her. Despite all the nice things that Fati offered me that night, I felt so frustrated—and not because of any impotence.

At first the newbie seemed to have had some experience with foreplay. As soon as we were lying in bed, she started wriggling around like a roused snake. I soon discovered, however, that she was like a silly goat, recklessly touching every intimate part of my body before I touched her anywhere. She kept sticking her tongue out like a chameleon hunting a grasshopper. She kept trying to fake how horny she was by biting my lower lip, scratching me here and there, digging her nails into my back like a crab, and moaning. I gently explained that I was not used to such a delirious type of arousal and that I didn't like it. She backed off and sat still. Then I asked myself whether I'd be able to do anything if I'd had a sane woman in bed. She must've been insulted when I asked her to stop trying to show off her sex skills. I know many men who are thrilled by bites, scratches, and pinches. They even brag about the marks on their bodies to prove how much they enjoy them. I may have felt a little sorry for the way I reacted to the newbie's behavior, and I probably could have asked her to be more gentle with her silly little routine instead, but that wasn't the first thing that came to my mind. The night wasn't all bad, but we lacked chemistry. Then again, it was only our first night together. Who knows?

It's beautiful when the rain falls, but it's a disaster when the drops fall through the roof into five buckets: plop, plop, plop, plop, and plop. I'd rather get soaking wet from head to toe than hear those drops splattering, which sounds as if a bird is pecking my head to build a nest or as if pins are being inserted into my forehead and eyelids. I don't mind if it pours on me in the streets or forest, but I couldn't stand the sound of that rain in my place. It was driving me crazy. It felt like Chinese water torture, but even though I was on the verge of going nuts and my brain was about to explode, I did not give up. The privileges of living on the top floor simply fell into the abyss.

I drank two glasses of wine, hoping to relax a little and go to bed, but my eyes stayed wide open, like an owl's. I didn't have anything stronger to help me get to sleep. I don't know how the newbie managed to sleep. I know people who can fall asleep in seconds, who don't need to plead for it. The moment I finally started feeling sleepy, her snoring got louder. It sounded like someone was choking while trying to whistle or like an old train was leaving the station. I didn't dare shake her, for fear that I'd humiliate her again. I don't remember how I finally fell asleep. I might have told myself that I was dead.

I hadn't gone to work in a while and must've spent all the money I had on drinks. I was in trouble. How would I pay Miss Newbie? What would she think? I remember paying for everything she drank that night. I might also have offered a few drinks to girls like her and men like me. I know how crazy I become when I start drinking with those damned people. I try to be generous so that they'll like me and think highly of me. I hate to brag like that! I scratched my head and beard and started thinking about how I should handle the newbie. She didn't look like she'd stolen money from me while I was asleep, the way other sluts usually do. She couldn't have anyway because Fati was our mediator. I must've lost the money somewhere or wasted it on something.

Ashamed and nervous, I offered the young lady an alarm clock, a can of sardines, a can of tuna, some apples and bananas, two pounds of Spanish rice, and a pair of shoes that were still in good condition. If she had a brother whose feet were the same size as mine, she could give them to him. I was glad to have found supplies with which to save the day.

"Aren't you ashamed of yourself?" she said when she saw what I wanted to give her. "Are you kidding me? You want to pay for the night with these things? We're no longer living in a famine!"

"That's all I have, miss."

"Save this stuff for when you're hungry. And for the record, I'm not a miss. I have a three-year-old daughter waiting for me to come home. You gave me a headache yesterday with your *miss* this and *miss* that."

"I don't have anything else to give you."

She lit a cigarette and started smoking it fast and on an empty stomach. So, she wasn't a newbie after all.

"Do you want some coffee?" I asked.

"How nice of you."

I couldn't tell whether she wanted the coffee or not. Her answer was ambiguous, but when she saw me going into the kitchen, she yelled, "I don't want coffee or anything else. I just want what I deserve: one hundred dirhams. Do you understand?"

"May God curse me if I own more than this," I replied with a shudder.

"What about last night, sir? Weren't you boasting about your money yesterday, reciting poems by Omar Khayyám, Abu Nuwas, and others? Poor thing! Listen, you promised me one hundred dirhams. Fati can attest to that."

I was flustered because Fati was the reason we had met. How could I face her once she heard about this mess? I wondered, even though I knew that she would believe I was broke and only gently blame me for it.

"I promised you one hundred dirhams?"

"Yes, Mr. Omar Khayyám," she said, using her first cigarette to light a second. "I've got clients who pay me three or four times that amount, but I accepted your hundred for Fati's sake."

I don't remember promising her that amount of money. She might have deserved it yesterday, but she definitely doesn't deserve it today. Today I can see how much of a phony she is. She was trying to hide her misery behind a luxurious coat, which was actually covered in moth holes and looked like it belonged to an old woman who passed away fifty years ago. She must have bought it from the junkyard or got it from another phony girl. I bet she never puts it on in the morning to walk along the boulevard. Her clothes were clean, but they smelled like junk. Her hygiene wasn't terrible, but the foul smell from her armpits made me feel dizzy and sick in the morning. She carried nauseating perfume, toothpaste, and a toothbrush in her faded purse. I wished she realized that the lavish look she cultivated was passé.

We had to go to the Petit Socco together so that I could borrow fifty dirhams from a friend who was working at Hotel Mauritania. If I couldn't get the money, she'd bang her head against a wall and curse me until the Day of Judgment.

"Walk in front," she commanded from behind.

I was afraid she might lash out when I handed her the fifty dirhams. "This is all I could get, miss," I said, then added, "Oh, Rabia al-Adawiyya!"

I was surprised to see her facial features soften and sprout like a seed. She returned my alarm clock, which she'd been keeping hostage, with a smile—as though she were handing me a souvenir. Her strong perfume lingered on the alarm clock. She might have assumed that I needed it more than she did. She refused to take more than thirty dirhams and, without saying goodbye, turned in the direction of Place Taqaddum, bit into her apple, and walked away. I was stunned as she kept going, not looking back even once. As soon as she reached the arch leading into the square, I disappeared. I thought she might turn to look at me one last time, as usually happens in such lousy separations. She played the role very well, but I don't like saying goodbye unless I have to. Goodbyes are tough, and the smiles that usually accompany them are usually not real.

I ordered black coffee at Café Tinjis. I had a terrible headache. It felt like I had cats inside my head, scratching each other and meowing. This bazaar—which every damned person, myself included, loves—brought me nothing but shit and misery. It even diminished the beauty of Café Fuentes. The square was a pigsty, filled with holes and shit. All the nostalgic memories I had of the place had vanished. I didn't even know the waiter who brought me my coffee. I could spot the readiness to commit a crime in the eyes of every person sitting or standing nearby. Anger filled their distorted faces. Horror filled those of the people crossing the square. I could see and smell deception. Where did those guys come from—the ones who looked like they had just gotten out of prison and were already ready to go back? They must be the kinds of people who—knowing they'll end up back in jail soon—would ask their cellmates to keep their favorite places safe. It was like a Tatar invasion. I couldn't have known more than three or four of them.

We've all gotten older, but life here is rotten and doesn't age gracefully. Even memory grumbles and complains, refusing to record any part of what is left. The skin of those who work permanently in the souk has not only shrunk and shriveled; it is also decomposing and covered with pustules. The fantasy of regaining their ancient glory is eating them up, turning them pale, and making them resent the changes that have defeated them in this blighted city—this corpse that hasn't yet been buried. The disease has reached the heart, a stroke from which the city may never recover. Its veins are torn out every single day, and it's going to explode!

> We do not know who is living and who is
>   dying
> We are all unlucky
> To still be here
> When the sun rises
> Radiant
> —*René Guy Cadou*

I walked up the sloping Rue Siaghine to get to Dean's Bar.
I wanted to drink some beer. It was after ten in the morning. I
must've been the first customer, because they had just opened.
The smell of alcohol and cigarettes was strong enough to make
you feel sick. I downed my glass in one gulp as a way of getting
used to the foul stench. Opposite the bar was a dark portrait of
Hemingway. It was clearly painted by a novice, but many of the
bar's regulars claim that it's a valuable piece of art and that an
expert would appraise it highly.

"The painter must be famous today," said an older patron
who considered himself the historian of the bar. "It's been here
for more than fifty years. It's unfortunate that the artist didn't
sign it. We miss out on a lot of opportunities when the greats, in
their humility, don't sign their work."

He wanted to see this Hemingway painting exhibited in one
of the world's famous museums. That would make the bar's
owner rich. Another client declared that he heard Dean himself
state that Hemingway was a friend, that he used to visit the bar
regularly when he was in Tangier, and that he'd always mention
how much he liked the painting. Hemingway was grateful to the
painter and wished him a bright future. He even wanted to buy
the art for more than the bar was worth, but Dean turned down
Hemingway's offer, preferring to keep the great painting as a
souvenir of their precious friendship, Hemingway's memorable
visit to Tangier, and his admiration for the bar and painting.

The bar's owner can no longer confirm or deny the stuff people are saying day and night, because he passed away years
ago. There are people who say that he's not dead, even though
he's buried in an English Protestant cemetery here in Tangier.

They even claim that he comes over from England or the United States every summer to commemorate his bar's anniversary. Everyone who's there when he visits drinks for free. There was also a small picture of Humphrey Bogart, the story of which is no less valuable than that of Hemingway's painting. Another old regular confirms that Humphrey Bogart personally donated the picture to Dean. The regular said he was there when it happened. He added that Humphrey was kind and generous, inviting everyone in the bar to drink with him. That older customer took pride in the fact that he'd had the honor of talking to and drinking with Humphrey—even if it was only once, when the actor was passing through Tangier. He had promised to return, after all, for another drink. The other picture on that wall was unimportant. It never inspired comment because its subjects weren't regulars, according to those who could identify the bar's entire clientele—old, new, and nonexistent. Nobody knew who they were or who brought the picture in to begin with. May God curse anyone who says otherwise! The picture shows a lady sitting in a luxurious chair, surrounded by attendants as she receives an old man. People have suggested that she's Barbara Hutton or a look-alike. But another art connoisseur had a different story.

"She's the leading actress in a movie that was filmed in Tangier," he said. "Tragedy struck this very city. A Spanish guy fell in love with a British girl who was from a family of diplomats. When she rejected his love for her, he gave up and hanged himself on a tree in her garden, right in front of her bedroom window. His guitar was dangling from his neck."

Nobody could ever confirm who the person in the picture

was, but everybody who saw it formed their own idea about
the woman's identity. It didn't really matter whether the people
whose pictures hung on that wall had really visited Dean's Bar
or not. They all existed in the vagrant memories of the city's
bargoers. The living subjects might be dead, the dead alive, or
neither one nor the other. It all depends on your mood, on what
you'd like or not like to hear. The subjects might be alive today,
dead tomorrow, and both the day after. Or they might not exist
at all, simply because no one in this bar or another had ever
heard of them or wanted to admit to having seen them somewhere in this miserable—but happy—city.

I was distracted by my memories of the bar, which had
been a shelter for foreign spies passing through on a mission
and elites living in the city back when it was an international
melting pot. Some names came to my meandering mind—Bur-
roughs, Ginsberg, Orlovsky, Kerouac, Bowles, Genet, and Tennessee Williams. No one at Dean's Bar ever talked about any
of them because their pictures weren't on the wall, and people
who voiced opinions weren't allowed to enter the bar in those
days. I wished there was a picture of even just one of the people
with whom I meandered.

I didn't intend to treat the newbie with such malice. I had
enjoyed her company at the bar. The worst thing was that her
kind and surprising behavior made me feel like a loser.

At the beginning of the seventies, women who had flunked
out of school began turning to prostitution. Malika, the newbie,
was one of them. Most of them used to come from other cities to
avoid bringing shame on their families, which might've brought
hatred and crime in turn. Lalla Chafika and her daughters didn't

feel that they were bringing shame on their families because they didn't have families. These new girls were desperate for a way out of their miserable lives; they weren't the fearless professionals who could stand up to anyone who tried to exploit them.

Fati and I became friends. She was the one who courteously initiated the friendship. Lalla Chafika gave it her blessing. I did not usually have intimate relationships with women, not because I didn't want to but because I didn't know how to initiate them. Women have always lived at a distance from me. They were always either sacred and untouchable or else soiled and dirty. I might also be afraid of women's need for control and their crazy jealousy, which can turn deadly. Why would I initiate any relationship when all I want is my own freedom?

Fati and I were no longer flirting the way we used to, except for the occasional caress or cuddle. We were more like brother and sister, but that was against my will because I still desired her as much as other men did. I wanted her to forget the platonic love she felt toward me. She'd overcharge the drunkards who lusted after her so that I could drink more than I could afford to pay for. I used to keep drinking for free so that I could stay there, with her, longer. She'd also offer me the drinks that crazy men paid for—her way of saying "Stay longer." And so I would drink more and stay longer. I'm broke and completely indebted to her. Sometimes my friend Zafzaf, who's just as broke as I am, sits with me.

The Inheritance

Exile.
I have been exiled twice
Once here and once
There.
Which one was stranger?
There's no choice
In the era of suffering,
Regardless of your homeland.
Only frogs do not leave their meadow.
What could I have said?
I'll leave tomorrow
But I was driven to do so
By force,
Surviving defiantly
Was so puny.
Here I am having left
And here I am having returned.
This is what I am now.

Hadi came back from the First Indochina War with his arms amputated. He knew why he came back, but he had no idea why he went.

He wasn't the only one to return with a permanent disability, but his was worse than those of the other people he knew. Their disabilities still allowed them to use the toilet on their own. He consoled himself with the knowledge that at least he'd die in his country. What if I'd perished there in the middle of nowhere? he thought. And become a feast for scavengers? That's the worst thing that could've happened to me. Hadi thinks that the way people die is a sign of either God's forgiveness or His curse.

When his wife died, their only son, Allal, took over the task of caring for him. Hadi admitted to his son that he was a more patient and compassionate caretaker than his wife had ever been. He would tell his friends, "I've never regretted having a son."

Hadi's wealth consisted of his French pension, a two-storied house, a piece of land, two cows, and a few sheep and chickens. His life was quiet. He didn't suffer from the anxiety or depression of old age or lament what he could no longer enjoy. His friends called him Hajj Hadi, but the only pilgrimage he had made was to the battlefields of a war that meant nothing to him.

Whenever he spoke to his son, he'd express a desire to get married so that he could spare Allal the burden of his care.

"I know what you want, Dad, but I won't allow it."

His father's desire to marry worried Allal. He was almost forty years old and had no professional skills. I should hire that kid to look after the two cows and seven sheep, Allal thought. I need to keep an eye on the women hovering around my dad. If one manages to seduce and marry him, she'll take everything.

Hadi suggested that his son find a wife; if nothing else, she could help take care of him. But Allal worried, What if the devil intervened? His father might desire her, she might desire him, or they might desire each other.

"I don't like that idea. I'm more than capable of taking care of you, Dad." Hadi was over sixty years old, but he was in good physical health. The only thing he'd complain about was the occasional bout of insomnia, and Allal never tired of meeting his father's needs, day or night. "I know you're only telling me half the truth. You're the one who's eager to get married, but you're ashamed to admit it. May God grant you a long life—but away from any woman, even an older one."

"A woman named Halima came over the other day," Allal told one of his friends. "She was childish despite her middle age and reeked of Arabian perfume, miswak, and henna. She claimed that she was volunteering to take care of my father in the name of God, but I kicked her out. 'Stay away from my father,' I said, 'or else I'll make you regret it.'"

"If your father insists on getting married," the friend replied, "pick out a wife for him yourself."

"That's my business. Keep your thoughts to yourself, or this friendship is over."

"Finish your drink and relax. You're right. He's your father, and I'm being nosy. I won't bring it up again."

"I know those old women," Allal said. "Who do they think they're fooling? The only thing they want is the inheritance; that's why they're all rushing to marry him. That would leave me jobless and miserable, forced to wander the streets. They're all descended from the devil."

What his father wanted was a woman with whom he could enjoy the rest of his life. Allal was aware of his father's flings; he'd heard about some of them from the man's friends. They had all grown old in the same village, and many—like his father—had lost spouses. But the widows were miserable.

Here's what happened or didn't happen.

Some of the women just talked to him, then left. Some talked to him, kissed his bald head, then left. Some kissed his bald head and the stumps of his amputated arms, then left. Others did all of the above and stood there amazed, looking at him until Allal came over, which was the cue for them to get the hell out.

Wicked barren women would kiss his bald head and his phantom hands, then throw themselves at his crotch to grab and kiss it. All that was left was for them to suck it and insert it in themselves. Allal would usually stay far away or pretend that he was not watching what was happening. When he went over to stand beside his father, they'd leave, mumbling things he couldn't hear. Maybe they were muttering words of gratitude, blessing, and good fortune.

One night, while Allal was having wine with his father, he wondered, What would happen if I did *that* to him? He might get mad at me, but he wouldn't survive without me.

Allal bathed his father once or twice a week in the morning with warm water, according to the man's wishes. But executing his scheme only seemed appropriate at night.

On sunny days he'd take his father on walks across one or

more fields, then bring him back home. He'd sit him down by the front door so that he could bestow his blessings on the people visiting him from villages near and far. His blessings had become famous among the region's women, both barren and fertile. Some would come to see him because they only gave birth to girls and wanted a boy; others would come because they only gave birth to boys and wanted a girl.

Has my father really become a saint? Allal wondered.

Widows and young women alike would flirt as they greeted his father, but Allal would always linger close by. If one of them spent too long chatting him up, Allal would move close to her. His silent demeanor in the presence of those women was dry, tense, and grim. He did not trust any of them—young or old. They were women, and for him, that was more than enough to justify his mistrust.

The same scenario played out whenever his father sat by the front door, bestowing his blessings. Allal was very firm with the women who approached his father. It didn't matter if they were old cocksuckers, young cocksuckers, or old cocksuckers pretending to be young. They were all the same to him.

Do they think they can fool me? he scoffed.

When Allal was with father's friends, however, he'd smile and join their conversations. He'd even allow one to have tea, coffee, or a meal with him and his father—either at their house or the friend's.

One night, when the sky was dark with pouring rain, Allal offered to give his father a bath. "Maybe a night bath will help you sleep better," Allal said. "I think it'd be better than waiting until morning."

"I hope so," Hadi replied. "Whatever you think is best, Allal. By now you probably know what I need better than I do." It would be the first time he'd bathe him at night. Allal drank many more glasses of wine than usual. He even put a bottle of wine next to him, drinking straight from it to control his shaky hands.

Allal was extremely happy as he scrubbed Hadi in the wooden basin with soap and a loofah. He had no idea whether his hellish plan would work!

He was telling his father stories about the village, but his father didn't seem to care much about that anymore. Hadi shared memories from his time serving in the French army and fighting in the Battle of Dien Bien Phu. The stories were short and often incoherent.

"One of my comrades was next to me," Hadi told Allal. "A grenade blew up his skull. His brain splattered all over my face. There was another soldier—I couldn't figure out how to put his guts back inside his stomach. I was utterly confused. Someone else came and solved the problem for me. Then the medics arrived, and the poor man lived."

Hadi told Allal—and others—the same stories over and over again, as if for the first time. The phrasing would occasionally change; he might miss a word here or there, but he'd never add a forgotten detail.

Allal held the soap in his left hand. Anxious, he slid it slowly down his father's body—the same way he slid it down his own during a dry spell, when he couldn't fall asleep without relieving the tension. His father's erection was a good sign, one that delighted Allal.

"Keep it up, Dad!" he said. "May God keep those hovering women, young or old, away from us."

It took only a little bit of gentle massaging for Hadi to start moaning in ecstasy. He was so horny. No words were needed. Allal was aroused too, probably even more than his father. It was a sensation that Hadi had not enjoyed since he'd returned from that damned war. Allal was sweating, but his shakes had calmed. After that bath, and the many others that followed, Hadi no longer brought up marriage. Allal felt that he'd be able to live a safe and serene life with his father.

The Pier

This was the fourth time that he made it to the end of the pier and was interrupted just as he was about to put his right foot onto the ship's deck. Someone was coming down in a rush and got in his way, so he stopped and turned back.

I sent him telepathic encouragements to push past the guy who seemed to have forgotten something on land. But they were in vain. I had bet on him stepping aboard this time. I cursed the guy, wishing I had been in his place to let damned Ricardo onboard.

Ricardo's obsession with returning to his dear home was stronger than he was. He must've seen an evil portent in that guy and thought to himself, I'm going up while he's going down? No way. We must go down together. He once returned to his apartment, canceling his trip, all because someone walking by his building spat. That damned Ricardo always backs out when he reaches the end of the pier, when he's halfway down it, or sometimes before he even sets foot on it. Then he turns back to go through customs, which have since become less crowded, yet again.

No Travel

It has become a habit of mine
To be the last to arrive.
I might be avoiding what is awaiting me,
Good or bad.
The long line
Always shakes my optimism.
I end up going back to where I came from,
Hoping never to return,
But I do return
And find more lines.
Every time I go, the lines multiply.
Getting to the front of the line is a miracle.
Wouldn't it better for me to accept my curse
And stay where I am?

The customs agent took me aside, keeping an eye on the inspections from afar. "What's going on with your friend? This is the third or fourth time that something has stopped him from traveling. Every time he claims he's forgotten something important in the city. Is he all right? What's this important thing he keeps forgetting, if you don't mind me asking?"

"His mother is sick. She's older, in her seventies," I replied. (She's actually healthy, with a strong personality that can face any illness or old age.) "He was born here and has always lived here, so he doesn't want to go to Spain just because he can't find a job in Tangier. The city's charm is what gives him the strength he needs to live a decent life. He doesn't know how to live anywhere else. He becomes desperate whenever he leaves Tangier, losing his taste for life."

I wanted to add that my friend is not exceptional, that I too find myself turning around and heading back to Tangier— whether near or far, at the very beginning of or halfway through my trip. But I told myself that one weirdo was enough for that customs officer; otherwise we might drive him mad.

"Is he also a writer? or an artist?"

"Yes. He plays the piano, but he's crazy about reading. He even reads while eating."

I was not exaggerating. Ever since he was a child, he'd read in the bathroom. He wouldn't open the door until his mom begged and begged, bribing him with promises to buy everything she had previously refused him. She did not always fulfill those promises, and to get back at her for denying his requests, he'd resume playing his game of defiance. And if he knew that his sister Candida was the one knocking on the door, he'd grow even more stubborn. "She can poop in her pants or on the porch," he'd say, "like that one time she had diarrhea." If his mom knocked and he surrendered only to learn that it was for his sister's sake, he'd snort and grumble, "Can anyone be trusted anymore?"

"He speaks Moroccan Arabic very well," the agent said.

"Yes, because when he was young, he lived among Moroccan children more often than among Spanish children."

I thought he might've been talking to me for longer than allowed, but the officer rank on his shoulder erased that idea. With a grateful smile he walked away.

We've run into each other at a few of the bars in town but never chatted. When we meet, he's bound to ask about Ricardo. He's very nosy—not, it seems, out of ill will but out of a fascination with the psychologies of weirdos like my friend.

I've wanted to write something about Ricardo for a while now. But the process of writing has stubbornly resisted. Every time I've resolved to write about people whom I know very well, the words have been blocked.

"Whomever you love, you may love more or less, as you wish."

I wrote that sentence, but I need to come up with something stronger and more attractive. That's not the way I should start my piece about him. Many writers believe that the beginning of a story is the hardest to write, but that's not necessarily true if you know how to court the writing's devil. As far as I'm concerned, the most challenging part of the process is finding a suitable title. The title should be as attractive as a peacock's crown or tail, or so I've been told by pedantic experts.

I don't know why something Cioran said came to my mind while we were in the taxi: "A poet who does not think about death can't be great."

We're used to respecting philosophers, but isn't it possible for a man to dream of something holy, knowing that it's futile? Isn't it possible to write just to dream, not to dream to save ourselves from the crushing damage that awaits us and others. I'm just wondering; I'm not against using writing as a means of banishing our fears.

"They inspected me more on the way back than they did when I was leaving."

"You've every right to cancel your trip, but they've every right to do their job."

"I'm sure that the officer who was speaking to you asked about me."

"Yes, and I told him you forgot your money and other important things you can't live without in Spain."

"Such as?"

"The spices with which you'll cook tagine."

I wanted to avoid talking more about his obsessive-compulsive disorder, which is what makes him turn around when he's boarding the ship. His behavior had started to raise the authorities' suspicions. They thought he was crazy, but they didn't think he was a criminal or a terrorist.

Ricardo feels affection for Otilia but only because he pities her. She suffers from anorexia. He might leave her once she recovers. That's what I inferred from the nasty way he was talking about her. His love won't last; it can only do so if he truly commits himself to her. She only ever eats one slice of toast with olive oil, a cup of jasmine tea, and a yogurt. If we insist that she eats more than one meal a day, she succumbs to our demands but then throws it all up soon afterward. That's the way people who suffer from this disease behave. In the presence of those who supervise their treatment—whether at home or in the hospital—they pretend to be innocent and obedient.

I thought that life's wisdom might draw us closer to death, which we cherish deep down, but I'm not tempted by death's magic carpet. I feel more like an heir to the misery of mortal life than like an heir to the bliss of immortal death. Death's wind embraces just a single season, whereas I love to embrace every season. Death is nothing but the death of the conscious self, so let me embrace all my seasons before they dissipate. I'm far removed from sura 44:27: "And comforts of life wherein they took delight."

Ricardo startled me as the car was passing through customs at the entrance to the port. "Do you suppose that my little piggy thinks of me when I'm away?"

"Probably. You don't seem bored with her either, even though she's kicked you out many times, as you've told me. Some people don't want to be loved by anyone when they're suffering from a chronic illness."

"That's true, but those people forget that there would be no Christ without the cross."

He'd surprise any stranger with the way he spoke about Otilia—as if the stranger knew her personally. He was prepared to provide many details about her nervous condition and give his opinion about their strained relationship.

"I don't believe in oppression that makes me feel the arrogance of eternity. It's true that Jesus created his life when he died. He was born to deepen human salvation through his own suffering, to confirm his message. But he was free to choose any other destiny."

Otilia was traveling with Ricardo in Málaga when she fell ill and took to her bed, awaiting death. He spoke less about her after she passed away, but his grief was just as mysterious as their relationship. It was neither a profound remembrance nor a superficial forgetting. It was something in between, something he himself might not have known. She died years ago but was only buried last year.

"What else do you want to happen to her? She was the living dead."

That was the last thing I heard him say about her.

When Ricardo starts talking about Otilia, you feel as though you're in a maze. It's the same when he talks about his mother, Alfonsina, the despotic tyrant.

"When I was young," he once told me, "she'd treat me in a severe and brutal way, the same way her mother used to treat her. She didn't want her daughter to face that oppression, so she showered my sister with care and love. She'd remember her mother and do her best to give everything she had missed in that relationship to my lucky sister. 'That's how you should've loved me, mother,' she'd say, 'the same way I love my Candida.' I never witnessed how cruel my grandmother, Rosalia, was. But why was I to blame? And who will take care of her now, whether I stay here or go to Spain?" (His strong attachment to his mother was another mystery, a blend of love and an extremely sensitive and boyish grouch.)

His mother lives alone. She employs a Moroccan girl to run essential errands. As soon as she asks her to do something, she pushes her gently aside. "Let me do it myself, my girl," she says. "You're still too young for this. Just watch me so that you can do it well next time."

"When the next time comes," Ricardo told me, "my mother will still do the tasks she assigns to the young girl."

Candida lives with her husband and kids in Almería. She

usually comes to Tangier once every summer, but sometimes she prefers to spend her vacation in Motril with her mother-in-law. Ricardo's maternal ancestors came to Tangier two years before the beginning of the twentieth century. His paternal family emigrated from Nerja during the French Protectorate. His maternal grandfather was the first to open a modern bakery outside the city, on the way to Sidi Bouaid. The village's gates used to close in the evening. Most of the inhabitants were Christians or Jews; their number was double that of the Muslims living there. A few Jews were of Amazigh origin. They were handicraftsmen, fortune tellers, and witches who used both black and white magic. They were refugees from Andalusia who settled there after Abu Abdallah Muhammad surrendered the keys to Granada and, as the Spanish saying goes, "wept like a woman for the kingdom he could not defend like a man." For every group of ten Christians and Jews, there was only one Muslim. Muslims would only pass through on Sundays and Thursdays, traveling from the countryside to Zoco de Fuera and carrying their merchandise on their backs or on their animals.

If a Moroccan woman, wrapped in traditional Arab dress, happened to hurry by, she'd grab the attention of the Christians more than that of the Jews, who spoke the same language as Moroccans and practiced similar rituals. Moroccan women would rarely go out, even in the city's alleys.

Delacroix, Alexandre Dumas, Mark Twain, Rubén Darío, Vicente Blasco Ibáñez, Pío Baroja, and Walter Burton Harris (a reporter for the London *Times*) all visited Tangier. The city's international fame, however, only began after the French Protectorate was established on March 30, 1912, and the revised

International Zone Statute (amending the Paris Convention of December 18, 1923) was ratified on June 12, 1928.

Ricardo's love for Tangier is stronger than his desire to visit his mother. He doesn't know how to break the spell that keeps him longing for that city. "Everyone who comes to Tangier," he once told me, "wants to deflower her without being her chosen lord."

Some of those people might be original inhabitants who miss the colonial era, despite its misery, because of how law and order prevailed in those days. No thief would ambush a man on his way home, threatening him with a sword or dagger—as now happens in broad daylight, right in the middle of the main boulevard. How can bystanders intervene? The people of Tangier used to be the city's protectors, but today they've turned into sadistic spectators who relish the spectacle of every bloody fight.

In 1993 I visited Nador. I hadn't been there for over half a century, since the mass exodus caused by the famine. The Elmas Association invited me to speak to an audience, and I read the first chapter of *al-Khubz al-ḥāfī*. The discussion was exciting and intimate among the young crowd but very unpleasant and narrow-minded among the older people there.

I remember our house, which was on the verge of collapse. I remember the scavengers hovering in the sky as my family migrated on foot to Tangier. I also remember the lifeless trees and the grim faces on kids and adults alike, both caused by the misery of drought. I was seven years old.

We tried in vain to locate people who remembered one of my father's uncles in the village neighboring Had Bni Chiker, known for its market. My mother was from the village of

Arhwanin. When the old man who guarded the village mosque seemed reluctant to remember my father's family, I thought that this might not be the village we were looking for after all. I had a strong sense that it wasn't right. I just couldn't find anything that recalled what I'd been told about it throughout my childhood. None of the people who had migrated from the village ever went back to reclaim their origins or residences. Those who did go back did so only because of their connection to the land (which they couldn't sell without being disgraced) and their desire to both reestablish relationships with family members who were still alive and pay their respects to the ones who had died. They would then return to the safe places where they had settled, reassured that no one—living or dead—would curse them.

The old man's tone showed not an ounce of regret.

"You must be feeling nostalgic," one of my companions said to me.

"Not at all. I'm just surprised that I was born here."

I appreciated his silence, which was probably more eloquent than any comment he could have made. We would've started arguing over the difference between real and false nostalgia, and that would've spoiled the rest of our interesting trip. How can there be nostalgia without the intimate memory of a place? At that moment reality and imagination blended together, and I was convinced that I would never return to look for my birthplace. Maybe I wasn't born here. I didn't even feel nostalgic enough to keep looking for that lost, hazy place. I may have been a child here once, but that *here* no longer meant anything to me.

The village was almost deserted. The fig trees were far away from us. The meadows were cloudy. There were young men smoking under an old fence. Small colorless houses. A group of curious and suspicious children kept looking at us; they stopped for a little while, then continued playing a game called "the dead horse," in which they took turns jumping on each other's backs. A barefoot girl was watching. My heart tightened, and I asked to go back to Nador. My companions seemed to understand how my mood had been unsettled since we started searching for the unknown origins of my father's family. Misery nested in the almost-deserted village. The present was so similar to the past! In the distance were some villas—newly built by the newly well-off, according to one of my friends.

Baba Daddy

Love affairs.
My love for you is eternal,
While all my affairs turn to dust.
"How did she respond?" he asked.
"She slapped me," I replied, "but then nestled in
    my arms."
"That's love in Tangier—impossible."
But then I said something I've never said before!

It is two o'clock in the afternoon. He rarely has more than two
or three customers at this hour; sometimes only one, sometimes
none. He'll enjoy a bottle of wine if he's on his own. Today he
cannot stop bragging about one of his customers, a regular at
his restaurant-bar in Bordeaux, who was a law student back in
the day and later became a distinguished minister in one of the
Moroccan governments. He called his business Bar Tangier so
as to keep his native city close to his heart while living abroad.
All the migrant workers and students considered Bar Tangier to
be their embassy, and Daddy their ambassador. His credentials
comprised the love they felt for him and the kindness that he
showed them. He even made them the dishes their mothers used

to cook. Each had different cravings, depending on what they grew up eating.

When the illustrious minister visited Tangier, he invited Baba Daddy to dine with him in a luxurious hotel, but Baba Daddy responded arrogantly—as was his custom when he had not yet had enough to drink. He was always haughty when sober, but he'd grow friendlier, funnier, and goofier around his regular customers once he'd had enough to soften up.

"He can come to my bar and have a toast with me," he told the messenger who presented him with the honor of the coveted invitation, "the way it was in Bordeaux, in the old days when we'd dream about independence and returning to our homeland."

No one had belittled him in any way, but he nevertheless launched into a tirade, going on and on about his past and future successes—in Bordeaux and in Tangier. The stream of memories conspired to upset and unnerve him. He'd have delivered a full speech if not for his wife, Dominique, who managed to stop him with her usual composure. "Daddy," she told him, "the nice gentleman is waiting."

In sheer astonishment the messenger repeated the time of the event and the name of the hotel, then handed him the invitation with a smile. Recovering his equanimity, Baba Daddy graciously accepted the invitation. He offered the messenger something to drink, but the man was on a formal mission and turned down the offer with an apology. A taxi was waiting for him outside, in front of his luxurious car, to guide him around town.

"I'm from Rabat," the messenger said. "I barely know my way around this beautiful city."

"You're welcome anytime," Baba Daddy replied. "As you can see, we crack jokes and have fun, like one big family."

The wise regulars who had witnessed that historic moment in Baba Daddy's life explained to him that the minister's status would not permit him to show up at a popular bar—regardless of its reputation—the way he used to when he was a student in Bordeaux. Even the regulars who weren't there to witness what had happened agreed. It was perfectly reasonable for Baba Daddy to abandon his pride and accept the minister's invitation.

This event could not be kept secret because Baba Daddy wanted everyone to know who Baba Daddy is and was.

By evening the news had spread, and the small bar was completely full. People who had been there earlier in the morning, and others who had not, crowded in. Even people who had had an argument with Baba Daddy came by to reconcile their differences. If it hadn't been for the witnesses, nobody would've believed him. The first round was on Baba Daddy, but he continued to drink on everyone's tabs. He got drunk eventually, and his voice turned hoarse with melancholy as he wept and sang old Tunisian and Algerian songs by Música, Saliha, Hassiba Rochdi, Sheikh El Anka, and Raoul Journo.

To mark the end of each segment of a song, he'd hit the wooden bar so hard that many glasses would shake, roll over, or break. Eventually he kicked out customers who were as drunk as he was—or more. They were all shouting "Long live Baba Daddy," hugging him and kissing his bald head. Those grown-up children, as he liked to call them, would've spent the night in the bar if he'd let them, but instead he shut the door in their faces. They were rowdy and smiling happily. He went up to bed because his dinner with the minister was scheduled for the next day.

Baba Daddy owned three suits. He hadn't worn any of them since he'd bought his big restaurant and little bar in the late fifties. The little bar was actually Antoine's, whose longing to return to his home in Bordeaux matched Daddy's nostalgia for Tangier. For more than a quarter century, Baba Daddy hadn't had any occasion to wear one of his suits, as he had regularly done in Bordeaux. Antoine's wife had died, and his three children had finished their studies and then stayed in their hometown, waiting for him to join them. Daddy didn't have any children, and his wife was very wise and healthy—discounting her obesity, which worsened when they settled in Tangier.

To commemorate the anniversary they shared, Daddy kept the bar-restaurant's name as it had been—Bourdeaux Bar and Restaurant. Everything went smoothly. Daddy didn't have to pay much to cover the sale price, as Antoine was fascinated by Bar Tangier in Bourdeaux. Baba Daddy and Antoine bartered like two brothers amiably dividing their inheritance. They had traveled to Bar Tangier together and toasted both cities. Dominique ran the bar better than Daddy in his absence, according to the testimony of their rowdy regulars. Antoine kept the name Bar Tangier to demonstrate his generous spirit.

Dominique ironed the gray suit and sprayed it with perfume to hide the strong smell of camphor. She hung it on a coat hanger at the restaurant and opened the front door, which had been locked ever since the economic depression had struck. Her hope was that the suit's weird and nauseating smell would dissipate with some fresh air.

"The smell's so bad," she told him, "you couldn't even sell the suit at a garage sale."

There wasn't enough time to have it dry-cleaned because such a fast service had not yet been imported from abroad.

Once they were in the bar's attic, which they had turned into a bedroom, Dominique reprimanded him for turning his encounter with the minister's messenger into a farce that had their customers boisterously and childishly cheering. Dominique did not normally have a lot to say, so she finished her scolding with "I'll go nuts too if you don't change."

He had to find something to say in his defense before they both fell asleep. He settled on, "I have the right to have fun with my friends as I please."

The restaurant was large. It was decorated with wooden and ceramic artwork that he had brought with him from Bordeaux. There was no sports decor in the dining room. His wife was not interested in sports, so he hung those souvenirs on the walls of the bar.

Daddy owned two pairs of boxing gloves: a first pair, which had not produced a victory worth mentioning, that he had taken with him when he emigrated from Tangier; and a second pair that was a memento of his knockout victory against an opponent in Bordeaux, or so he claimed. He lived between honesty and prevarication, exaggerating and embellishing the most mundane things.

The first pair of gloves was surrounded by two pictures: One was of Ismael Stitou, who gave up boxing at the right time to avoid an embarrassing defeat. He now owned a small nightclub that attracts customers from other bars, as well as some suspicious figures. The other was of Abdeslam ben Buker, who was less fortunate and still waiting in Tetouan for a rematch against his opponent Kid Gabellan. Kid Gabellan had defeated Abdeslam more than fifty years earlier, in Cuba, in a world championship for which Abdeslam was not qualified but in which he was pushed to participate for business reasons. He returned home defeated and suffering from a neurological disorder. It was said that something had been put in his drink before the match.

The second pair of gloves was surrounded by two pictures: One was of Joe Louis, who won fifty of the fifty-four matches he fought, forty-three of which resulted in a knockout. The other was of Muhammad Ali, known as Cassius Clay before his conversion to Islam. In the corner, by the entrance, was a picture of Daddy posing as if he were in the middle of a boxing ring before the first round. The background of the picture revealed that it had actually been taken in a photography studio. Another picture showed him in his twenties; and another, more recent, in his seventies. He had insisted for years that he was sixty-seven, as if revealing his age to some stranger who happened to come into his bar.

Baba Daddy rarely made any money off the restaurant. Every order had to be placed at least one day before it could be picked up. The city had been facing a tourism crisis since the War of 1967. Then came the Gulf War, which put an end to the faintest hope of reviving the damned economy.

Baba Daddy did not allow people to drink in the restaurant unless they ordered a meal or at least an appetizer. Moroccan women were not allowed inside unless they were accompanied by a man and looked respectfully modest. He wanted his restaurant to keep the reputation it had garnered.

Dominique was in charge of managing the business accounts. She sat in her office at the restaurant's entrance and never got involved in the bar's affairs. She kept her poise, gaining the respect of customers. Even Baba Daddy would speak to her succinctly and quietly when he was walking by her office. There were very few customers whom she would greet and with whom she would chat. She always had a glass of wine under her desk, which provided a convenient excuse for turning down someone's invitation for a drink. Baba rarely let the waiter who helped him at the bar serve her. He would bring her a glass himself and silently remove the empty one.

"What prolongs a relationship between a man and woman," a customer observed, "is the few words they exchange!"

Daddy was a boxer in his thirties. Before that, when he wasn't yet twenty, he sold newspapers. He was also proud of being the first Tangerine communist. When Franco, who was called Paquito here, seized power, Daddy joined the Republicans. Those who were arrested in the northern region rarely returned home. Executions were taking place daily in this city and elsewhere. Tangier's international status shielded its Republican residents to a certain extent, but the terror that Paquito spread in other cities still seeped in and even intensified. Paquito's supporters and spies outnumbered his opponents. His motto was Fascism Is Also Democracy, though he was an even worse dictator than either Hitler or Stalin. Paquito was not only afraid of intellectuals but also despised and executed them. What were people supposed to expect? The best-case scenario was to be imprisoned in El Hacho, Ceuta's horrific prison, just as horrific as Alcatraz. Every so often, scores would be settled outside the city or in its alleys at night. The Rojos (communists) and Fascists would shoot or stab at each other. Sometimes they would call each other names and end up exchanging gunshots in the square between Café Fuentes and Café Central. The bottom line was that emigration—with all its risks—was more compelling to young Daddy than staying in the city to fight Paquito's supporters.

Daddy migrated to Bordeaux via Oujda and Algeria. His comrades, the Rojos, lost a very important member of their cell when he left. He managed to save himself by leaving Tangier at the beginning of May 1940, before the city was seized by Spain on June 14 of the same year under the command of General Asceno of the Mehal-la gendarmerie.

In 1953 I was working as a waiter at Reqassa Café in the morning and selling contraband cigarettes at night, right after the daytime sellers left the Petit Socco. Daddy used to come at least once a year in his Chevrolet or Dauphine to visit family and Tangier itself—the mother of all Moroccan cities—when it was still in the prime of its youth and glory, so much so that some considered it to be part of Europe.

He was always elegantly dressed in shiny shirts and luxurious pants that he changed more than once a day. He was very popular for being stylish. Daddy knew what colors to wear and how to match them to the season during which he visited, his height, and his Viking-like blond hair. He was one of my regulars in the morning. At night (his night, that is) he'd don his fugitive garb and go to brothels looking for the prostitutes he'd known before he fled overseas. He'd discover women expelled by the Spanish Civil War. Jewish prostitutes from Eastern Europe were his favorite; they used to welcome their clients into their tiny houses in the Oued Aherdan neighborhood, the doors always wide open until dawn and the windows covered with dark curtains. They stayed there even after the Nazis were defeated. He also liked Andalusian prostitutes because he hadn't visited Spain since leaving Tangier before the cursed Paquito's occupation. He was only ever interested in French prostitutes when desire overwhelmed him; whenever he returned to Bourdeaux, they always expected him to bring back their favorite Moroccan souvenirs, such as embellished slippers, caftans, silver bracelets, necklaces, kohl, and henna and its wooden applicator. Their New Year celebrations were always more festive when he returned before New Year's Eve, as he'd ship their gifts before his arrival. His love affairs with them usually ended in bloody fights, during which he'd knock out his troublemaking French or Algerian rivals, even when they were carrying switchblades or were accompanied by one or two more guys.

"Can you imagine a boxer needing to use a weapon?" he would say. "What an insult!"

As for Moroccan prostitutes, he'd spend the whole night with one in his favorite hotel—the old London Hotel, whose rooms had wooden floors. He'd order the oldest Spanish wine and either beef tagine with prunes, almonds, and hard-boiled eggs or lamb with local potatoes and olives, cooked under low heat on charcoal from either the Rihani or Hammadi restaurants. Both were close to the hotel, unique, and unparalleled in the quality of their Moroccan cuisine.

On one of my evening strolls I stopped to drink what I could afford: one glass at Jacobito and another at Bar General. I ran into Daddy in front of the new mosque; he looked enraged and defeated, as though he had fought three or four people. He was drunk, and his face was all scratched up. Thrusting his fists into the air, he kept threatening to suffocate and kill "her." "She" must have been Fama, the Casablancan. Daddy could lift her over his head using only his left or right hand, but as puny as she was, she could make him kneel in front of her and surrender to her seductive, fatal, gypsylike caprices.

"Have you seen her?" he asked.

"Fama?"

"Yes."

"I saw her a few moments ago. She was heading toward Nasriya Street."

"With whom?"

"With a young guy," I replied maliciously, solely to amuse myself at the sight of his anger.

"That bitch! Screw her! I'll kill her tonight."

This was not the first time he was going to bury her alive.

Flowers of the Dead

Tears invade me
Through my thoughts.
Maybe feeling weak made me think of myself
Or of someone else.
Crying is not just crying.
Sadness may shy away
From itself sometimes
When it conquers the oppressed.
There cannot be peace with murderers.
I steal moments
Of stray joy.
My self-confidence may have worn me out.
Today's depression may be born of the past;
Its languid forgetfulness does not liberate me.
Who can bring back our glorious gatherings
In the bars destroyed by the Tatars?
Those bars that kept us happy
As we shared our sorrows!
Is it our despicable age or our miserable fate?

The time will come to state,
"Neither this nor that."
What is over is over.
And whetted hope will return
To its niche.
What hope is there
If it is nursed by despair?
Words may sadden us and not gladden us;
They may be somewhere in between—
One word
Or the other.

You are the ever present, only able to rescue itself.
You have had your time, and after you, I will have
    myself for me.
I won't say that I'm lonely
Witnessing the damage.
Beauty can be glimpsed through its mirage.
Is it sadness? misery?
Or is it miserable fate?
Perhaps you and I can recall
How she and you yielded to
Memory's embrace.

When the world drowns in blood, Tangier will only sink to its heel. That's what Sidi Bouarrakia said and what later became the slogan for Baba Daddy's bar.

He was sitting near the kitchen, relaxing in an armchair that he had bought a while ago, specifically for taking naps. He was an old man now, and he had just started acknowledging the way that his age was taking a toll on his pride. He tried hiding it, but it was obvious to everyone. Only humor could overcome his ego, but he reacted to people's jokes with caution.

He was half-asleep when he looked at me. His tiny blue eyes were partially hidden under his eighty years, but they lit up whenever someone started an interesting conversation. Nobody asked him to talk about the years he had kept for himself. He no longer responded to the jokes about his age. "What do you care what my real age is?" he'd ask. "You're all just nosy and horrid. I've come to regret knowing some of you. You'll be shitting your pants and beds when you're my age. May God grant you all good health, even if each and every one of you is vicious."

"Aaah, there you are! Welcome."

I sat across from him, in the corner by the entrance, beneath his photograph. He still looked young in that picture, wearing boxing gloves and on guard. His wrists and ankles were swollen. He'd been suffering from gout for years, though flare-up were rare. Maybe he'd just worn himself out that day, during a training session with his former students, trying to convince the people who joked about his age that he could still put up a fight. On one occasion Mohammed Berrada came with me to see him. We found him sitting close to the entrance, wrapped in a blanket. He showed us the swollen fingers on his left hand.

"That's what my ring's done," he told us, "because I haven't taken it off for more than forty years. I sent it away to get fixed. It was a gift from Dominique the day we opened this bar."

His voice was faint. The best thing about him was that he rarely whined, and if he did complain, he never exaggerated.

Maybe he considered sadness to be intimate and personal. He had over sixty years of experience drinking, mostly with wine and beer. It was rare for him to drink strong liquors like tequila or absinthe, which he used to drink excessively in Bordeaux and then quit. He'd only make an exception when a retired sailor who was living in Gibraltar came to visit.

He had not shaved for days. He probably didn't remember how to shave properly, or else he did remember but had become lazy and was neglecting his appearance. His hands were shaking as he had his morning drink. On a small table next to him sat a beer without a cup, as usual.

I did not have the shakes yet, unlike him. I could still enjoy my breakfast, drinking cold beer and savoring the scent of the day's first cigarette. Smoking made me cough a bit but did not make my eyes turn red or tear up. I knew that my turn was coming, though. Baba Daddy was taking his pills and acknowledging their effectiveness, even if they never managed to stop his indulgence in drink.

"Everything has its place in the body," he would say. "Medications have their place, and so do food and drink. Everything else is pure superstition."

Karim came out of the kitchen carrying a vase of lilies, which Baba Daddy's late wife, Dominique, used to love. He put them on top of her desk and then covered the bouquet. She could not have children, so she had adopted Karim when he was only a baby. He hadn't once visited her tomb since it was built.

"Go to the bar and stop being a hypocrite," Baba Daddy said to Karim in a weak, irritated voice. "She isn't buried there."

The office stayed empty; even Baba Daddy didn't use it. "I

won't have it any better than her when my time comes," he said, "but that doesn't make me sad. I'm not expecting any of the damned people spawned by this accursed world to mourn."

I raised my index and middle fingers, and Baba Daddy agreed with a nod.

"A beer for him and another for me," he said to Karim. "Okay?"

"Yes," I replied. "God bless you and make you prosper."

He has started talking to himself a lot in recent years but has still managed to stave off senility. Karim brought us our beers. Mama Dominique adopted him around the same time that she encouraged Baba Daddy to marry a Moroccan girl forty years younger than him. Dominique wanted him to stop having affairs. She also wanted him to be able to have kids with that girl. And so it was: he had three children—two boys and a girl—with her, just as Dominique had wished. They are still in school today. The girl is more studious than her brothers, according to Baba Daddy. He never spoils them, but they know how to get around him when he's in a good mood. Karim has quit his studies and gotten into sports.

When Baba Daddy fired the bartender, Karim took his place.

The economic crisis was getting under the skin of every small business owner. There was still life in the city, but its glorious golden era was gone. Tangier lost its fortune, yet its spirit was ever present. People who went bankrupt used to comfort themselves with stories about the winter, which retained only some of the spoils of the previous summer. No one wonders how Tangier can be saved. Its legend feeds the silence that envelops it, as we wait to see what happens next. Its legend is stronger

than its history. What distinguishes it is the fact that, despite
the clash of civilizations in its midst, it has never entirely lost
its soul. Anyone can practice Judaism, Christianity, or Islam in
the spirit of peace and tolerance. Some of those who saw the
city back in its heyday remain, but most people today only see
its bygone glory. In an unskilled attempt to turn the city into a
legend, they have dissolved what was left of its sturdy heritage.
From the way I was moving my right hand around my eyes and
gesturing with my left to Karim, Baba Daddy understood that
Karim was in tears. He was sitting at the far end of the restaurant hall. Baba Daddy called to Karim without leaving his seat.
Karim came over, wiping his eyes. Baba Daddy handed him
fifty dirhams. "Go buy the flowers that she used to like and the
flowers of the dead. I forget what they're called, but the florist
will know. Visit her tomorrow—or whenever you feel like it—
assuming you can remember where her grave is. Maybe I'll go
with you."

Magdalena's Face

Jealousy.

I see what I see.

I may like what I see,

But I cannot

Live what I see.

Perhaps.

"No woman deserves you but me," she said.

"You're not the only woman out there," I
    replied.

"How old are the others?" she asked.

"They're of a similar age, more or less," I
    replied.

"Are you close to her?" she asked.

"Some things bring us close," I replied, "and
    others keep us apart."

"And in between?" she asked.

"Sometimes it's me," I replied, "other times
    it's her, and still other times it's neither of us."

"I don't believe anyone," she said.

The face of Magda—or Magdalena, as one of her Spanish lovers used to call her—changes three or more times every day.
Magda is the name she keeps for herself, though she may reveal
it to one of her close friends in an intimate moment. It doesn't
matter if it's her real name. As a way of exalting the name she
kept hidden from us, we called her Mother of Goodness. According to Arab linguists, the Spanish word *mujer* (woman)
may well be derived from the name with which we honored
her—*khair*, goodness.

I imagine that if Magdalena stays up or goes to sleep late
and then wakes up early, her morning face has a lemony or oily
hue. After she's had a nap, however, the color of her face turns
orange. And in the evening it glows brightly.

I remember Magdalena's bright face, back when she was
younger than twenty and the marines' ships would regularly
visit Tangier. If you dared speak to her then, she'd behave like
a tigress being harassed by an unwelcome mate outside of the
breeding season.

Magda, Magdalena, or Mother of Goodness came from
Tetouan in the late fifties with her mother Zahra (or Zhiru, as
her girlfriends nicknamed her affectionately). Among the Spanish and their soldiers, she had a glorious reputation as a whore.
She's retired now, but there's no genuine repentance.

Magdalena (as she and her Spanish lover preferred) or Mother
of Goodness (as we liked to call her, even during the dirtiest pe-
riods of her life) rarely slept with Moroccans—whether men or
women. One of her flings was with a gypsy, so she sometimes
incorporated gypsy words into her Moroccan dialect, which she
spoke with a southern Spanish accent.

She had a long face, a nose like Cleopatra's, and lips the size of a large diced strawberry. The rest of her was more or less attractive, arousing us whenever we wanted to have a good time with an ordinary woman whose limited beauty would probably not last beyond her youthful days.

One day in a Sevillian bar, I asked to sleep with her.

"I don't like fucking Moroccans," she replied arrogantly.

"Why?"

"Because they don't pay well and they're brutal in bed. They might kick and slap me without paying anything. One man spat in my face when I asked him to pay what we'd agreed. They consider themselves machos, and foreigners effeminate."

Years later the marines' boats only visited occasionally. Their pockets were no longer bulging with cash. By the end of the fifties, the international brothels of the Petit Socco had been closed and very few Spaniards still lived in Tangier. In the 1940s the Spanish began turning the streets of Tangier into their home. Having gotten a taste of living there, many refused to return to their neighboring country, even after the Spanish occupation ended on October 11, 1945. For them, Tangier was a paradise when compared with Franco's Spain.

Magdalena was getting older and so was I, so I thought there was no harm in asking again whether she'd sleep with me. She didn't respond. The bar was empty except for two prostitutes whispering to each other. The older of the two kissed the other intimately. I envied them that delicious kiss and longed to be between them.

Magdalena started ordering one glass after another for herself and the two lovers, all on my tab. I let Magdalena exult; it was her day. She wasn't telling stories or jokes as she usually did. From time to time, she let out a sigh, then absentmindedly inhaled the smoke from her cigarette. I detest that self-destructive type of smoking. She was smiling, then frowning, and then brightening up again. I expected her to explode into hysterical laughter, but she didn't. She just kept on ordering drinks for herself and her colleagues at the bar. I kept quiet, not wanting to appear stingy.

I was worried about her absentmindedness and silence. Did she think that I was trying to retaliate? Embracing her body was all I had wanted in the past and all I wanted today. No longer was I obsessed with her body—its softness; its protruding breasts; its prominent curves, bends, and folds; or its harmonies and symmetries. What interested me now about Magda, Magdalena, the Mother of Goodness, or whatever other name she wanted to use was how much I had longed for her the day that she rejected me. Pure sex—that might have been all I wanted on that particular day. But now I crave the warmth of my yearning—a reminder of past loneliness or of a desire to embrace a body with love or hushed touches, to feel the presence of a body next to mine and know that I exist. That would be either a remedy for the past or the satisfaction of a desire today.

She grabbed my hand hard.

"Shall we leave or stay longer?" she asked me, with an expression that was strangely inviting.

"Whatever you want," I replied. "The evening's yours; I'll only take from it what you lavish upon me."

"You're wild. Come with me."

She smiled and ordered two more glasses for us and a third

for the girl she was inviting to drink with us. Neither today nor tomorrow mattered! It was all about my desire and hers, ours together. Who desired it more? Who desired it with us? Nothing mattered.

I surrendered to her dismal yet delightful desire. I didn't feel like I was degrading her. It was enough to make me want to go on the pilgrimage with her. Neither my past with her nor her present with me mattered. I wouldn't have any dates with anybody on any other day, even with someone I loved. There would be lust and love on some days, love and lust on others, and lust without love on still others. But there would come a day when the two poles would attract one another and fuse together. That's how I felt with Magdalena in her home.

She showed me a room inside her house, which was on the verge of collapse, in which she had perfected the art of decor. I imagined that such decor would suit only those who wanted to lie in a bed of roses. The decor might be just for her, or it might be for her and her companions.

I had no idea what her morning makeup would look like, before she had her coffee and first cigarette, before her coughing began, and before she smoked three or four to stop it. I kept picturing her as women I knew who were like her.

Sagging flesh had begun invading her body. Her skin folded here and there, everywhere but under her knees, where we trembled from touching each other. Her face, oblong in my memory, was now covered with wrinkles, which have no mercy on those who are addicted to wakeful nights.

Our attraction wasn't feverish, but it wasn't devoid of attempts at giving pleasure either. I surrendered to her in a mysterious way, and she to me. I sensed that a Tatar conquest was imminent. It might have been that she didn't really want to sleep with me, to preserve her sense of pride as in the old days. Maybe she only surrendered because she needed the money. Maybe the glasses of cognac and the cigarettes had softened our moods. That was the last night we spent together. She teared up at first, but then we both had a good laugh. We became friends. I did not ask her why. Maybe there were beautiful things that we wanted to share, or maybe there weren't. Would words have helped us? Were we too proud to use them, or did we just want to keep them to ourselves? It was our business, and we promised each other that we would never reveal anything.

We used to meet at the restaurant El Dorado. It wasn't a big deal if one of us didn't show. No one there—or not there—had the right to ask about what was going on between us. It was just my face and Magdalena's, two faces in one.

Hamadi the Gambler

I gamble
To win, even if only a little.
That is one of my virtues.
The sea! Oh, what a sea!
From it we were born and to it we shall return!
The sea is our mother, not our father.

He whispered these words only to himself and to his fans, who loved this city, embellished by the color of the sea and licked by its foam. Between its past and present lies a lost paradise.

Hamadi the Gambler was interested more in the thrill of winning than in the amount involved. Sometimes winning turned into a vindictive act. Playing with him was characterized by hatred, hostility, and a sort of hidden violence, especially toward those who had beaten him before. One night he won a gold chain from a player against whom he held a gaming grudge. He was afraid that he would lose against him and be forced to give it back, so he cut it into pieces and flushed it down the toilet. Neither friendship nor empathy had any place in gambling—that was his belief. He'd play recklessly and stubbornly to satisfy his pride, which dictated that he always win. He wouldn't leave the gaming session—whether it was held in a café, a bar, or one of the professional gamblers' houses—until either he lost everything or the other players were all almost broke, making him the biggest winner.

He was obsessed with the people in this city knowing him as the infamous gambler. It didn't matter if he was winning or losing. Gambling is impetuous, and it was the only way he could prove his worth.

On the road to bankruptcy, he was infected by gambling mania. In some of his delusional episodes, he'd order two beers or a bottle of wine and two glasses—one for himself and the other for either his opponent or his alter ego. Whether he won or lost, he'd celebrate each game by drinking both glasses. Sometimes he'd rebuke his alter ego for his loss, going so far as to insult himself. "You should've played that card here, you stupid pig!" he'd say. "And that one there, you idiot!"

He was overly generous when his winnings multiplied. He distributed his gains—whether they came from his alter ego or an opponent—to the wretched boozers who had reached the bottom and still kept on drinking, seeking refuge in Tangier's ephemeral glory days.

Every time Hamadi won, he'd say his opponent's name and, raising his glass, shout "You lost, my boy!" He couldn't help himself when his opponent—real or imaginary—had previously defeated him. "Oh, yeah!" he'd boast. "By now you should know who you're playing with, boy! Don't kid yourself into believing you'll always win."

Hamadi chose his imaginary opponents with extreme care

in order to sharpen his gameplay. He based his choice on either their skills or how many times they'd defeated him by sheer luck. Some were cheaters—or alleged cheaters. But Hamadi cared more about competing and fighting with the other players. He'd allow a cheater to cheat as long as he was the sole arbiter of honesty and deceit. That would add some excitement to the game, balancing seriousness with pure fun.

The games would often start in the evening and go until the morning. Whenever he got tired of playing, he'd pick an argument, even a small one, so that he could withdraw at the perfect time to get some sleep. The players who were in the lead usually insisted that those who wanted to withdraw stay until the very end. The real gamblers avoided Hamadi after he went broke. Those who continued to hover around him were penniless too—whether more or less so didn't matter. No one could tell whether he was actually bankrupt; sometimes he'd have a huge amount of money. No one knew where he got it from. Did he inherit it? Was it a loan? Or was he winning somewhere else?

As a child Hamadi had had a passion for playing marbles and tossing heavy Spanish coins into a hole from far away. No one could match his skill. When he didn't have enough coins or marbles, however, he'd get frustrated and lose. In exchange for more marbles or coins, he'd pull his pants down below his knees for everybody to see. Such a trade was common among teenagers. Sometimes, however, they'd have to look for grown-ups with a kink for boys just to keep the game going. Trading with those human-crocodiles was more lucrative. The barterers

weren't embarrassed, knowing that there would be both winning and losing days.

Everything in this world became the subject of wagers:
whether it would rain, drizzle, or neither, that day or the next;
whether the sky would be cloudy or clear; whether there would
be lightning, thunder, or hail. This evening Hamadi the Gambler placed a bet on the time of sunset and lost. Yesterday, however, he had bet on the specific time the moon would rise and
disappear and won. Sometimes he'd gamble alone, without
even imagining an opponent. We had no idea how he could win
or lose against himself. Yet when he played El Solo, a game
for single players, we'd hear him blame himself for misplac-
ing his cards. When he played against himself or an imaginary
opponent, he'd usually bet only on drinks. But sometimes he'd
throw in some coins, and if he won, he'd give them to someone
he deemed deserving of charity—to spend on gambling, drinking, and sex. He never placed bets on sunrise or sunset until
daybreak because sleep would always defeat him.

One day he was tempted to stay up all night to win a huge
bet on both the sun and the moon. His friend, with whom he'd
been close since childhood and in whom he now placed his
faith, supervised Hamadi's every move to make sure that he
didn't fall asleep. His opponent woke from his deep sleep a
loser. Amateurs rarely played that particular game. Rumor has
it that Hamadi the Gambler invented or at least popularized
it. Hamadi used to gamble every day during the holy month
of Ramadan, from its beginning to its end, except on the
Night of Decree. He'd be playing, winning, and losing in all

sorts of games until the moon retreated and the sun took its place.

As long as Hamadi found someone willing to take his bet, he'd never miss an opportunity to gamble on the sun and moon. Such opportunities were plentiful during Ramadan, so he could play with real persons instead of wagering on imaginary stakes. Perhaps the fact that alcohol is forbidden during the holy month made people gamble, smoke hashish, and practice sodomy (which aroused fewer suspicions and cost less than sleeping with a prostitute) even more.

Days before he died, he was seen sitting on the stairs facing his bar, which was famous for the quality of the food it served during the city's glory days. Even such delicacies as pigeons with rice and grilled sparrows were widely available. He personally shopped for the groceries, including meat, fish, pickles, and snacks both savory and sweet. The bar was well known to the city's residents, as well as to tourists from other Moroccan cities. The only sound you'd hear was Umm Kulthum's voice. Photographs of her, taken at different concerts in Egypt and elsewhere, decorated the bar's walls. There was also a picture of the late King Mohammed V and of General de Gaulle.

The reason he went bankrupt was that he refused to pay taxes, which kept accumulating. He was sent to jail but got out thanks to a generous businessman, the head of a cigarette-selling dynasty, who cared about the bar's reputation. Hamadi did not learn his lesson, however; he continued spending every penny he got on bets and homosexuals. By the end of spring, his bar was demolished. Rumor had it that a pharmacy would take its place. He used to sit down in front that bar and, drinking directly from a bottle of wine, play cards with his alter ego or an imaginary opponent. Every smash of the demolition set his heart racing.

"There's no shame in building a pharmacy," he'd tell his former customers. "That's a good deed. People will be cured, but my bar healed a lot of people too. They'd enter my bar feeling nervous and exit as calm as ever. They'd enter as misers and exit as philanthropists. It wasn't always like that, though; more often than not, people would be harmless when they arrived and criminals when they left. They'd start plotting their crimes in my bar and execute them outside. I was lucky that not a single crime took place inside my bar; otherwise, it would've been shut down just like the others."

Hamadi the Gambler was married to his bar. He existed through it. Many suffered emotionally when he and his bar went bankrupt, because they felt just as alive there as he did.

The food that he used to serve with each round of drinks, whether fish or meat, had its own magical taste that was out of this world. The strangest thing was that neither the type nor the quality of his bar's food was affected by how much he was losing or gaining from gambling. He knew what he was doing, as people said.

Hamadi the Gambler did not always bet on what was universal or all-encompassing. Sometimes he'd grab a bunch of miswak twigs, which we use to clean teeth, and ask in his betting voice, "How many do I have in the palm of my hand?" If a customer left the bar, he'd bet on whether the guy would come back or not. He used to bet on the train's arrival time and its delays, on soccer games and all kinds of sports, and on the number of dead people to be buried in the three religious cemeteries. He didn't even spare the dog graveyard on Boubana Street. Maybe the strangest thing he ever did was to bet on whether someone could fart three times in a row. The person in question did in fact fart three times and offered Hamadi three more as a souvenir of his brave bet.

Hamadi the Gambler's madness knew no limits. He became an object of entertainment even for people who hated gambling. One day he went to Marshan Cemetery with a gambler who was as crazy as he was. At noon he bet on the number of dead people who would be buried during the Asr prayer, and he won. He also bet on the number of children who would be buried that day—not during any particular prayer, since innocents don't need to ask for God's forgiveness. "They've left our earthly paradise to join the eternal one," he said. "From God they came and to Him they shall return; the devil does not corrupt them. I've lost because I shouldn't have bet on their souls." That mistake tormented Hamadi the Gambler; he began to fear children and feel guilty whenever he saw one.

People said that he inherited a fortune from his brother, who had been extremely stingy. On Hamadi's deathbed, however, he confessed sorrowfully that his brother had left him peanuts in comparison to what he had left his late lovers. That is why Hamadi had decided to squander it all. He had gambled madly and lost everything he owned to two fierce gamblers who had exploited his drunken state and sadness over his share of the inheritance. He and his brother used to sleep with the same boy, who was either from the city or new to it.

Rumor had it that he was feeling extremely depressed and distracted one night after losing a lot at the bar. He may have been drunk as well. As he was crossing the railroad tracks, he lost his balance. A cargo train was passing by in silence and struck his head, which was tilted further forward than the rest of his body. He died in the hospital.

Solitude

I dream,
I dream until the dream replaces
The dream
And I finally see what I'm dreaming about.
Love exists,
But conversation is personal.

In the train compartment was a woman, her daughter, some guy, and me. I saw the man raising his left side to let one rip. Holding my breath, I quickly opened the door, took my small bag, and exited into the corridor. A fart rarely nauseates me, but the one this bastard released was on an entirely different level. It smelled as if he'd eaten a frog or half a dozen eggs and hadn't gone to the bathroom for days. The woman and her daughter also came into the corridor to look for seats in another compartment. She looked at me, and I could tell how astonished and distraught she was. I responded with a nod of solidarity, displaying my disgust for what had just happened.

As the train was approaching the station, I thought to myself, This is Asilah, my stop. Goodbye, Rabat. This was not the first time that I had traveled on the basis of a beautiful whim. Last year I had canceled my trip from Rabat to Cairo because I began the day by eating an omelet with rotten mushrooms. It was then that I realized that my hotel room was number 13 and that I was supposed to travel on the thirteenth of the month. To make things worse, my dog Juba was sick and dying, so I went back to Tangier. No travel under circumstances like those!

I walked back to the city. It was still too early to go to the Three Amazonian Sisters restaurant. They were all equally kind. Two of the three sisters worked there as waitresses and used to give me a special look to indicate where I should sit. The eldest was always in a good mood, except during her time of the month. My bag was light. I headed for the beach. Ahmed was there, walking slowly with his arms behind his back. I stopped him because we hadn't seen each other for years. The last time we had had a drink together was at Café Pilo. How many times had I bet myself and others that I'd see him accompanied by someone else! But I never won that bet. He worships his loneliness. He shook my hand loosely without saying a word. He only ever shakes hands with the tips of his fingers, and those to whom he entrusts his handshake should consider themselves lucky. We smiled at each other, then started walking contentedly. The worst thing you could do was startle him with a conversation. You had to lay the groundwork before speaking.

"How's Tangier?" he asked without even looking at me, as though talking to himself.

"I'm still living there," I replied, "but I no longer know what's new in the city. I only go to two or three coffee shops and my apartment, whose ceiling hasn't collapsed on me yet. I no longer cling to my old habit of wandering through its alleys."

"You've gotten old, then!"

"It's the city that's gotten much older than me. They've mummified it!"

"Who betrayed whom?"

"We've repudiated each other without breaking up."

"Disloyalty is necessary; it refreshes affinities."

I knew that Ahmed often walked along the beach or went to the Cave of Pigeons, passing by the Jewish cemetery. He used to walk miles and miles a day unless he was stopped by heavy rain or big storms.

One day near the end of autumn, we were sitting on the sand, shaded by a rock. The sky was cloudy, there was a gentle breeze, and the sea threatened to turn rough. He reached into his bamboo basket and grabbed a bottle of wine, a small glass, olives, Arab cheese, and whole wheat bread that his mom had baked in their neighborhood's traditional wooden oven. He shared his food with me. We talked a little about fishing in Asilah and how it had retained its simplicity. We also talked about how it was safe to walk around at night and go wherever you wanted. He no longer went up to Borj Krikia to drink his bottle of wine because the place had become crowded with young boys who would sit on the edge of its walls and talk all night.

> Lone I muse but feel not lonely,
> Covert solitude's my lore;
> For my company I only
> Want my thoughts and nothing more.
> —*Lope de Vega*

These words describe Ahmed's rituals, according to his brother Khalil.

Ahmed retired early, either because he was no longer any good at teaching or because teaching no longer did him any good. In any case, he suddenly resented doing his official duties. Anything obligatory was repulsive.

He still has a room in his family home, and he's the only one allowed to enter it. His four brothers got married, while he stayed single and continued to live with his mother. A solemn silence persisted between them. She learned the Quran and Hadith by heart and had a unique sense of traditional culture. Even though she was approaching her ninetieth birthday, not a single gray hair showed on her head. It was the same for her children.

His three daily meals were strictly scheduled: breakfast was at nine, lunch at one, and dinner at nine. If the meals were served slightly earlier or later than their prescribed times, he would leave the food outside his room. He'd protest this unacceptable oversight by going out and eating at one of the local restaurants.

"What happens when he gets sick?" I asked his brother Khalil.

"We can't tell whether he's sick or not sick because he never complains about anything or asks anyone for help." Khalid continued, "He usually throws his leftovers outside the house so that we won't find out how much he's eaten or whether he liked his food. One time he screamed in the middle of the night. There was a loud commotion. Our mother went to check on him but stayed by the door. He kept his room's door open day and night. He was sound asleep. The table was overturned; he must've kicked it during his nightmare. Some of the things on it—an empty wine bottle, two glasses, and a carafe whose contents were unknown—were broken. He was the only one who cleaned the room, and he never left any trace of things that had been broken. The mystery of the second cup is still unsolved to this day. He doesn't always leave it on the table. Sometimes he fills it up and leaves it there for days before emptying it, then repeating the process all over again. None of us ever dares speak to him. We greet him in silence. If he's in a good mood that day, he may respond to our greeting with a glance or a nod. The light in his room is a faint red, and he doesn't turn it off at night. He doesn't read or listen to the radio, but we used to call him the bookworm before he started dissociating. Even his library has since disappeared. The RCIA radio is all that's left in his room, but we have no idea whether it still works because he doesn't use it anymore. You could sense, even when he was young, that he was absorbed in his solitude despite being constantly surrounded by people."

"And what does he do when he's all alone in his room?"

"He meditates, smokes, and drinks his wine without making a fuss. He doesn't wait for anyone and doesn't want anyone to wait for him. Sometimes he'll disappear for days, and we won't have a clue where he's gone—whether he's stayed in a hotel in the city or traveled to Tangier, which he's loved for ages."

Ahmed had been feeling alienated from his city for several years. There was love from a distance, but the conversation was forever personal.

His brother Khalil claims that his solitude was a choice and not an illness, as some might imagine. He once dived into the sea and disappeared completely. Everyone watching assumed that he wouldn't emerge, but then he started floating and diving again. Soon they all spotted his slim figure standing on the beach.

The only conversation that people saw Ahmed have was between him and Cherif El Majdoub, who used to smoke one cigarette after another, including the filters. El Majdoub only asked people he knew for cigarettes. He always rejected cash. Rumor has it that, when he was young, he was a real stallion with women. He had a third foot, as they put it. One of the girls, the one who was craziest about him, put a spell on him because he left her for a Spanish girl. His Moroccan lover lured him into spending the night with her; when he left her house the next morning, he was completely out of his mind.

The encounters between Ahmed and Cherif El Majdoub never lasted more than a few seconds. No one knew what they said to each other. Ahmed smiled, but El Majdoub had forgotten how to smile since going crazy. People said that they had been childhood friends.

They once saw Ahmed scold Aicha El Majdoub because she had flashed someone who was harassing her. She showed him her butt, cursing him and his family. Ahmed sympathized. Khalil had his own share of weirdness that even surpassed his brother's solitude. He is a gifted painter, but he took the plunge into the unknown, perhaps because of some trauma he suffered. He exhibited his work for the first time in the late sixties. There was a clear theme running through the pieces: living skeletons, ghosts awaiting burial, crucified and hanged bodies, and other beings who had lost all human features. His paintings were confiscated the next day. From then onward, he stopped painting human figures and instead illustrated symbols of their existence. His paintings were never polished, signed, or sold, even though his meager teacher's salary was barely enough to live on. He would gift his paintings to friends but only if they asked or had a mediator ask on their behalf.

People who wanted to buy his paintings were upset at his unwillingness to sell. An exhibit was organized in his honor in Switzerland. He not only refused to sell, as usual, but also abstained from explaining the purpose of his art. An atmosphere of frustration and puzzlement prevailed, but there were some who understood his beliefs and respected him even more for them. Still, he couldn't avoid criticism for his Don Quixote–like personality.

"What will become of your art?" I asked him once.

"Oblivion," he replied. "I don't really care about its fate."

He used unconventional and fragile materials in most of his paintings, like soil, indigo, and perishables.

I knew Khalil in the late sixties. I saw some of his paintings but never asked him for one personally or through a mediator. We are now in the year 2000, and the only painting I ever got from him was by another painter. I've never seen anything more trivial: an oriental belly dancer lying on a bed. The painting was not framed, so I nailed it to the wall. It stayed at my place for a few days, then one night I folded it up and threw it from my apartment's balcony into the street.

We used to meet occasionally, by chance, either in Tangier or Asilah. Neither of us was looking for the other. He didn't like to drink on his own. He wouldn't refuse if I invited him for a drink—whether in a bar or at my place—but only on the condition that we each paid for ourselves. I couldn't figure out how Mehdi convinced Khalil to cover most of the bill. Mehdi was a skillful and crafty magician. (I won't deny that I too was his victim more than once, but I became aware of his tricks and started retaliating in my own sweet ways.) I didn't know about Mehdi's secret ways of luring people in. I had my own sneaky techniques, to which idiots can attest.

"I despise overdressed people," Khalil told me one day. "I despise obese people who overeat."

It's my good fortune to be neither one nor the other. Khalil looks just like a ghost to me. He's not of this world.

Women

Cunning and Other Falsehoods

I learned in a hospital in Majorca that the owner of the Granada Pub had fired Fati at the onset of the economic crisis because profits had dropped significantly. Even the international smuggling barons of Tangier were shaken. The crisis also rubbed off on the unsuccessful election candidates, who had wagered huge amounts from their filthy fortunes on winning. Some were partially paralyzed as a result, while others suffered heart conditions or nervous breakdowns. Small business owners went bankrupt and developed ailments—insomnia, malnutrition, intestinal disorders—just as terrible as their losses. The smell of sewage reigned supreme in popular districts. Downtown streets could not escape the foul stench that seeped into them or the horrors and crimes that continued to escalate.

Fati's rivals, both men and women, speculated that the real reason behind the Granada Pub's bankruptcy was money being swiped from the cash register. Fati was for the first time publicly dating a handsome lover, who lived on her dime. He pretended to be her protector, but he was the one in need of protection— from the old gay men who were bankrupt and very dangerous. How could he possibly fend off the infatuated advances of those whose hidden inclinations and desire to shower a jobless, spendthrift sweetheart with gifts were awakened by his beauty?

Construction started at the bar to transform it into one of those fancy tea lounges that were popping up all over the place, one after the other, like a fungus at the base of every building. Sometimes a new tea lounge would open its doors, while the apartments above it would remain uninhabited for months or years. People believed they were only built to launder money.

"They want to transform the city into a Moroccan Paris, while it's struggling just to crawl out of the drains of misery that are making it stink and drown."

"But all the lounges are full every evening. On the weekend you can barely find a seat—morning or night."

Some people thought that Fati's dismissal was a cover-up for a new development in her and the bar owner's lives. They were seen together many times outside the city, talking intimately for hours in his car. It was believed that she had been his secret mistress ever since she began managing the bar. The bar owner would later declare his genuine repentance, after he suffered a series of disasters: his son died in a car accident, his daughter went missing for months, and he almost died at the hands of a bunch of glue-sniffing teenagers armed with kitchen knives, penknives, and razor blades. Today he's one of the city's philanthropists, contributing to the construction of mosques and the promotion of national celebrations. His influence on Fati is clear: she donned a hijab and started to live according to a "this is permissible and that is forbidden" mentality. She also tried to influence other girls to behave like her. The man was therefore rewarded twice: once for his own repentance and once for hers.

In order to redeem herself from the sins she had committed—
from the day Lalla Chafika brought her from Larache to the day
of her repentance—she had to cut ties with all the whores she
had known.

"How can she snub her sisters like this?" people asked.

Some of her former clients from the Granada Pub started
calling her names and spitting in her face because she had
stopped returning their greetings.

One summer morning, she met two such whores and tried
to persuade them to seek repentance and embrace, in this filthy
age, the precept of the hijab. The two girls had just left some
random hotel. They hadn't slept much with their clients, so
they went to one of the morning bars that welcomed those who
stayed up all night. Some cold beers would calm their nerves.
The heat had set on very early that day. They walked past Fati,
looking at her as if she were a buffoon. She spat a bitter insult
back at them and continued on her way, mumbling to herself.
But the two girls went after her and assailed her with kicks,
punches, and scratches until she bled. Her headscarf fell to the
floor, her hair was ripped out, and her *jilbaab* was torn from the
neck to the chest. She began begging for help, shouting pite-
ously like a clucking chicken. She had never been in a physical
fight like that.

"One girl would've been enough to take care of her," someone remarked.

Each girl, however, wanted a turn at biting, beating up, and
getting revenge on the old apostate whore, as the two assailants
and other girls had taken to calling her. It was clear that they
wanted to settle a score with her, as she had been the one to call

the shots at the Granada Pub, deciding who could and couldn't get in. Cars were passing by, and the noise of the traffic was getting extremely loud. Some drivers were slowing down so that they could watch what was happening. Men gathered, enjoying the scene, as she tried in vain to protect herself. The women who were present disapproved of the unequal fight and begged the men to stop it.

"It's a dirty fight!" some of the men said.

"You're all just standing there watching!" a woman shouted. "This is what you all want."

The men finally intervened and pulled the girls apart. "It may be a bitches' spat," they joked, "but two against one just isn't fair."

Sweet, generous Fati spread various rumors about me for reasons I'll never know. She claimed that I was her father, in love with and planning to murder her. When she rejected me and I persisted, she threatened to report me to the authorities, so I ran away, claiming insanity so that I could take refuge in a psychiatric hospital in Tetouan. To mitigate the scandal and preserve the dignity of her beloved family, which she had inherited from Lalla Chafika, she got married last summer to a migrant worker living in Denmark. He too had sought repentance from God, also at the hands of the bar owner, with whom he had shared a strangely intimate childhood. He demanded, as a condition of their marriage, that she cut all ties with Lalla Chafika. That was after he discovered that the woman smoked and drank, unwilling to repent. He told Fati that there was no reason for her to grieve over Leila and Yasmina, as the girls were not her real sisters and were living with Lalla Chafika anyway. When Lalla

Chafika found out about her fate, she cursed Fati and her husband, as well as the day that destiny had enjoined her to raise
abominable kids she had not given birth to. She thanked God
that she hadn't brought any of them into the world. If she had,
she'd have cursed herself too and gone crazy by now.

She Comes Back

We may meet.
Imagine falling for your lover,
Perhaps for a moment, for a day,
For a part of your life.
No one ever witnesses
How it starts or how it ends.
I remember that our path
Was one,
But distance separated us:
I am at its furthest point,
And your are at its nearest.
We may meet or never again.
I had to see you the following day
To travel together or stay together,
But I had left some of my clothes
At my grandmother's place.
I promised her something that only grandmothers
Cherish.
Ask your grandmother,
Because they're all alike in what they love.

I usually drink two or three Alexander cocktails at Café Madame Porte whenever I can afford them. Salvador, the bartender, is very skilled at preparing them. His expertise also extends to dry martinis and Manhattans, which I prefer to drink in the summer. People say that Alec and Evelyn Waugh shared their cocktail-making knowledge with Salvador.

How strange! It's her, in all her elegance. Her square face is chubbier, appropriate for her age, which is now close to forty. More than fifteen years have passed. What strikes me the most is that her blond hair looks even more blond to me now than when she left. Her skin, which was the color of wheat when she left, is now almost white. The only thing she's missing are the lovely rosy cheeks of white girls. After expensive plastic surgery, the scar on her left cheek has disappeared. Her owl-like eyes are still attentive, eager to see everything at the same time. She sits by the bar's entrance. Her focused gaze and the shadow of her dubious smile drew me toward her. I imagined her thinking to herself, Will he agree to sit with me? She stood up, and we hugged.

"I was told that this is your favorite spot," she said.

"Sometimes," I replied. "The good old days at the Granada Pub vanished with you."

She smiled, then asked, "Did you believe the things people claimed I said about you?"

"Enough time has passed for me to forget."

"Everything said about us was just a rumor. You know Tangier's whores better than I do. Their envy is lethal, and their rivalry savage."

She has every right to redeem her past since her future is now secure. As if she had never been one of them, as if her bottom lips had never suckled the same milk! My alter ego, who always exercises control over me in moments such as these, stopped me. I wondered, Have you come here to renew this friendship or to fight?

"Fati," I began.

"Yes?"

"The things that were said about us are mere trifles, mere jokes, to me. You now have a new life in your new guise, and I have mine. The people who said what they said may still be busy gossiping about others or confined to their homes, or maybe they've migrated or died."

"I heard that you've written some books."

"I wrote a few after I'd liberated myself from the curse of pencil pushing."

"So, you never really liked your job?"

"What about you? Did you like the work at the Granada Pub?"

"My job was different. I was a slut and a bastard, with no roots. That's what they used to call me."

"Does it still hurt?"

"I've had plenty of time to get over it, as you just said."

"It's the same thing. Curses exist in every job. Even writing books has its share of curses, abuse, and assault—to the point of harassment, imprisonment, and assassination. Actually, I may have suffered more insults than you. People have spat on me in the streets, in bars, at official and nonofficial institutions—everywhere—because I'm a damned writer."

The waitress came over. I ordered a Bloody Mary, as Fati had done, because I enjoy its spicy flavor.

"How did your husband die?" I asked.

"In a car accident. He was working in a bakery, and I was working in a cafeteria. I flew him back here a few months ago so that I could bury him next to his family."

"So I was told."

"I had to go back to Horsens to deal with the insurance paperwork and our pensions."

She relaxes; her smoking is less nervous now. Maybe she thought that I was going to attack her. She takes a sip from her drink and licks her lips, toying with her car keys. No doubt some new type of harassment awaits her, involving those men who knew her at the Granada Pub and those who knew her when she wore the hijab. Tangier is worse now than when she left. I don't think she can defend herself. The snake that was long asleep is now awake.

"I arrived a few days ago," Fati continued. "I'm staying at the Hôtel Bristol. I want to find an apartment for rent or purchase soon. I can't stand living with my in-laws. 'How much of his salary did they leave you?' they keep asking me. 'How much do you expect to get from the accident insurance company? And what about your joint account, how much do you have in it? We're certain that you have plenty of money. The deceased wasn't a spendthrift. He didn't drink or smoke. He didn't have any vices. He was a pious man both here and in those Christian countries. Isn't that so? You've both been working for more than fifteen years. If it weren't for his help, we would've died from hunger. He—God have mercy on him—helped us every month, more than necessary. We'll be depending on you, our daughter, from now on. You can see how we're living.'

"They have even more questions about my plans now that I've come back. It's his mother who has taken on the task of interrogating me—not her husband or their five children, three of which are unemployed: two boys and a girl who has just broken off her engagement. Another son works at a junkyard, and the last is a fisherman. If I'd stayed with them more than three days, they would've poisoned me. They realize that I have no family left after Lalla Chafika died. They want me to become one of them so that they can inherit everything I own. They're hoping I become the lover of one of their unemployed, drug addict, or married sons, or else the wife of one of their relatives, who have rushed to see me from near and far. I'm the widow returning from a rich country."

"What about Leila and Yasmina?" I asked with a sigh.

"They were with me in Marbella. I haven't heard any news from them for years now. I don't think they want me to know what happened to them. I realized from their letters that I abandoned my family when I got married. I helped them in whatever way my husband allowed. Maybe the three of them were right. My marriage was a false ambition. When I got married, I couldn't recognize what was happening because I was going through a period of weakness and heartbreak."

"I saw Lalla Chafika once in the Zoco de Fuera," I told Fati, "and another time near the corniche. She was panting as she spoke. She complained a lot about her sickness and old age. But I never heard from her again. Both times she was very sad."

Fati's eyes filled with tears, and she stood up. I avoided mentioning how she, Leila, and Yasmina had failed to help her and how she had died alone and miserable.

"Come visit me in my hotel if you feel like it. There's a hall and a bar. Or maybe we can meet here tomorrow. I'm going to have dinner at El Dorado. Come with me if you feel like it, or join me later."

"Not today. Maybe tomorrow."

I remember the day when I asked her to marry me, and she turned me down.

"I spend more on my family than you make in a year," she told me. "You'd be marrying a family with four members, and you'd be the fifth. You have to wait until Leila and Yasmina finish their studies."

Her marriage had broken down her resistance. For my part, I was just going through a capricious phase. Once again I was sick and thinking about marriage. It was only later that I realized that I was looking for a nurse, not a wife.

I found her sitting in the same spot. She looked more tense than yesterday. I again ordered the same drink she had—a Bloody Mary—to counteract the cold February air that I had brought in from my hour-long stroll. Her features made it clear that she had not slept very well. When the waitress brought my glass, Fati downed the rest of hers and ordered another. She stubbed out her cigarette in the ashtray and lit another. She was taking deep drags and exhaling only a little. Her pallor overwhelmed the makeup she was wearing. She was furious.

"What I wasn't expecting has started," she said nervously. "When I left the parking garage near my hotel yesterday, someone was there waiting for me. He shook my hand calmly and kissed me on the cheek. The bastard did that so as not to raise any suspicions. He'd never kissed me before."

"What time was it?" I asked.

"Around ten o'clock. He snatched my purse, smiling all the while. Someone else was approaching, so he returned my bag. 'Don't you dare make a sound!' he told me. 'One scream, and you die.' Once the other man passed us, he took the bag back and emptied it of all the money it contained—more than one thousand dirhams. My checkbook was in there as well. I wish he'd forced me to sign a blank check. That would've been my opportunity, but he wasn't that dumb. 'Are you planning to live alone at our late brother's expense?' he asked. He returned my bag again, now staring at my gold ring, my necklace, and my earrings. 'Repent again—that was the reason my brother married you. Get remarried before you resume your old habits, from which my brother saved you. I'm familiar with all the places you frequent, day and night. Our entire family knows what you do there. Be reasonable. We will punish you severely, showing no mercy, if you don't ask for God's forgiveness and help us financially.' I thanked him with the same fabricated calm he was using on me, then asked if I could leave. 'Have a good night,' he said. 'Think carefully about what I've said. We're here if you need anything.'"

She left, thinking to herself that Tangier had become a place that drove those it trapped to suicide. Everything fabulous and wonderful was long gone. It wasn't clear to her then that what she had just grasped was in fact what she wanted and needed to know.

I could not think of anything to say to her, so I lit a cigarette and ordered two more drinks. I almost told her that the Bloody Mary was delicious but that it got you drunk fast.

"What do you think?" she asked me. "I'm confused, humiliated. I won't be able to live here like this. Now I'm regretting coming back after sorting out my paperwork in Horsens. Living there is tough as well. Everything's very different from the habits and ideas I brought with me from here. The frigid weather penetrates your very bones."

"Then go to another city, like Marrakech," I replied. "Living there is very appealing and comfortable. The city has maintained its authenticity, and its people are fun."

"If I stay in Morocco, they'll find me—no matter where I go. Their sense of smell will track me down unless I cross the border. That's the only thing that'll lead them astray and make them abandon their search. It's my fate to live abroad. I'm thinking of moving to southern Spain. I've never had the chance to visit the cities there, but we drove by them when my husband and I returned in the summer to vacation with his family. I've heard a lot about the joys of living in Spain since Franco's death."

A toddler approached us, trying to walk straight. He looked at her, then at me, then at her again. She touched his hair with a sad smile. He gave me a look as though he was imploring me to take care of her. He went back to his mother, who was sitting alone, smoking and relaxing. She greeted us as she was leaving, and we greeted her back. The child said goodbye with a dreamy look, not yet knowing how to smile at strangers. I don't know if he could tell the difference between men and women.

I ordered two more drinks without asking her. I knew that she had come here to drink, perhaps to get over yesterday's shock. She lit a cigarette. She hadn't lost much of that determination that had defined her personality at the Granada Pub. She knew how to fix the things that she regretted and how to start over before falling apart.

"Did you ever drink in Horsens?" I asked her.

"With my friend Chastine, on her birthday and on New Year's Eve. She had lived in Tangier for a while in the late seventies. She was a hippie and the only friend my husband let me spend the night with. He admired her. We knew her family. But I smoked cigarettes during work. I knew that her brother had a crush on me, and I let him. My husband and I no longer had much to talk about. We'd used up all the memories of our homeland and hadn't adjusted to life in Horsens yet. I wanted to adjust, but my husband only allowed me to talk to some of our neighbors. I'd spend some time with them on weekends or play with their kids. We didn't have children, so our neighbors' were like our own. He was very kind with them as well. In the evening he would pore over his religious books, while I would either watch TV or read one of the Arabic books that I brought back from every vacation."

She started stuttering a bit. She'd utter a word, pause, then move on to the next. She was getting drunk and giggling quietly. She did not let her sadness overwhelm her. She had matured. She was so relaxed that she was crying cheerfully. She wanted to order two more drinks.

"It'd be better to have them at my place," I suggested. "I have stuff to drink there. I still live on the same street, in the same stork-nest apartment on the top floor."

"We'll leave after these," she replied.

I also get stubborn about drinking whenever I'm distressed. I suggested that she leave her car parked in front of Café Madame Porte because it was safer there than in front of my building. She was wobbling a little, so she held on to my arm. Our walking together wasn't suspicious, but people who knew me kept giving us curious looks as they walked past.

"I only have wine," I told her.

"Give me anything," she replied.

She emptied her glass in a single gulp as soon as I poured it. She was completely submissive, enjoying her nakedness under the sheets. Twice she went to the bathroom wrapping herself in the sheets and looking just like a walking statue. The third time, the sound of her vomit was like that of a cow about to be slaughtered. I moved to the bedroom. She acted haughty, as though she were the queen of closed doors from the era before her grandmother, who had died a century ago, was born. She was struggling to hide her malaise. Sinking into the bed, she lay there shivering, which made me shiver as well. Her perfume filled the air, and her hands were ice-cold. She was still in good shape; nothing sagged yet. I don't think her husband ever explored these areas of her bodily geography: hips, butt, legs, earlobes, and spine. I don't think he ever touched her nipples; it would surprise me if he'd even sucked on them. She was aroused by her hibernating desires, as though she were a virgin.

In the morning, it was my turn to throw up. Bloody Marys are merciless when you overindulge.

She left me a note that read, "I didn't want to wake you. I'll have crossed to the other side by the time you get up. I'll write to you." She signed it "Your scared cat."

Her attacker was watching as she parked her car in front of the hotel and went inside. When she came out again she was with a member of the hotel staff, who was carrying her big suitcase. She saw her attacker approaching and signaling that she should wait for him. She started the car. The porter had already put the bag in the trunk, so she tipped him and left at an insane speed.

Her attacker followed but arrived too late. He must've had trouble getting into the port. She gave him a mocking stare as she rested her elbows on the ship's railing. He froze. "Bastards!" she said to herself, then walked away.

A letter from Fati.
From Marbella.
I remember what you told me:
When you visit a city
Don't ask after anyone.
You'll meet the person you'll love.
You may or may not know him.
That's the way it was.

She is wiser now.
The restaurant owner is a widower.
He has two sons, and so does she.
She is now the mother of four
And a father's daughter.
He is her father's age.
She works in the morning,
And he works in the evening.

A husband, kids, and a restaurant.
How happy her exile!
To be so lucky.
How miserable the return.

The Death of a Hippie Fish

It may bring you happiness
To listen to your favorite song,
But turn it off if it makes you sad.
To wake up in the morning
To a bright sky,
But go back to bed
If your dream was better.
To hear the phone ringing
When you already know who's calling,
But do not answer if it's going to put you in a bad
    mood.
To cancel your travel if your dog is
Dying.
Who has owned a dog like yours?
To leave before the end of the funeral
While listening to a joke.
Don't you have the right to ride a donkey?
To hear crazy giggles and hold firm.
Don't you have the right to stay or leave?
No one blames you on your day,
If you created it.

Maybe your craziness involves people you meet in the
    morning,
And their craziness involves people who meet you in
    the evening.
For a mother to hear her mute daughter sing,
Even if she herself is deaf?
Yes,
Someone has to sing.

Farid comes to the bar at the end of each month. There he
spends the part of his salary that he reserves for himself; the
rest goes to his family. He stays until evening, then goes back
to Larache. He may spend the night if he doesn't waste all his
money inviting the bar's regulars and prostitutes to drink with
him. Sometimes he doesn't even know them.

At Bar Negresco he'd often find someone to drink with,
someone to put up with his boring conversation and his frequent gripes about his family. The regulars, to whom I introduced him, were used to his monthly visit. If he failed to find
any regulars or passersby willing to sit with him, he'd start a
monologue with a small black fish, staring at it with childlike
wonder. He named it Nadia the Hippie.

"Farid!"

"Yes?"

"Why do you call it a hippie?" I asked.

"Can't you see how long its hair is and how thick those little
hairs are around its neck and gills?"

"And why do you call it Nadia?"

He gave me a silent smile.

He hadn't changed much since I knew him in the mid '50s. He has always been hesitant, doubtful, insecure, and dependent on other people. He is incapable of hurting a fly, except during fights with his wife, Yamna. She always starts a fight for the dumbest reasons, cursing him in her Rif dialect, which he doesn't understand. He can tell, though, that she's cursing him in front of their kids and neighbors. Yamna taught the dialect to their eldest son, but the poor boy doesn't dare translate a single word of what she says for his father.

When I insisted that he marry Yamna, I was hoping that the marriage would help him get over his addiction to masturbation, which exhausted his skinny body and twisted his mind. I thought that he'd give her two or three kids for her peace of mind. Instead, his wife-rabbit gave birth to fifteen children, and a sixteenth passed away only one hour after the child's birth. When I asked him about this madness, he blamed his wife and absolved himself.

"She's the one who refuses to use any kind of contraception," he told me.

Even now I don't consider Farid to be a sane person. He fluctuates between intelligence and stupidity. He suffers from an obsessive-compulsive disorder that causes him a lot of stress. To relieve that stress he guzzles what's left of his beer, grasping the bottle in one hand and tapping its bottom with the other to ensure that he gets every last drop. His behavior provokes guffaws or glances of pity, depending on the regulars. But this never happens when he's at Bar Negresco with me.

My approach to make him deal with his illness is to keep quiet and not worry about what he says, instead of telling him to stop acting the way he does. This technique makes him realize how uneasy I feel, which makes him abandon his obsessive behavior shyly and apologetically. We'll then sit in silence until, all of a sudden, he breaks the ice and lures me back into listening to whatever he has to say. He doesn't care if my comments are right or wrong. He believes in my opinions and never questions them. I don't like his blind, passive attitude. He disgusts me, but how could I put an end to our friendship?

Whenever he had money left, he'd stay overnight at a cheap hotel. At night he'd frequent the bars that attracted whores. He'd offer them drinks, though all they drank was his smell. He didn't care if his escort was actually drinking. What mattered to him was how entertaining her stories were. If she couldn't tell a good story, he'd look for someone else. The more he was moved by the story, the luckier his escort would be. He'd buy her more drinks and sometimes tuck money into her pocket.

Farid also felt more relaxed when his escort knew how to listen, sound sympathetic, and sigh. He knew that he was being fooled but played along so as not to ruin the night. He never took any of his escorts back to his cheap hotel, no matter how beautiful and attractive they were. He treated them like his sisters, just as he treated shoeshiners like his brothers. I had the impression that he's wasn't confident in anyone's affection but theirs. Perhaps some type of masochistic feeling possesses him and ties him to their world.

I was having breakfast when the doorbell rang. It was Farid.

"That's it," he told me as soon as he had sat down, without preamble.

"What?" I asked.

"I've moved to Tangier. I'll teach in one of the primary schools."

"Where?"

"In the Bni Makada neighborhood."

"Why did you move?"

"The kids are all siding with their mother against me. Last time I argued with her, my eldest son got up and violently grabbed me by the collar. If she hadn't freed me from his grip, he would've hit me in the face. He insulted me, spat on me, and threatened to kick me out of the house for good."

"Things could've been worse. You aren't the only one."

"You're lucky."

"How?"

"Because you've never cleaned anyone's butt just for them to humiliate, beat, and insult you. I'll get away from them."

"You have an army of kids. They'll follow you wherever you go. It's more expensive to live in Tangier than in Larache."

"I'll figure it out. I'm just asking you to let me stay here while I look for a place that I can afford on my salary."

This had to be the dumbest thing he's ever said to me. I drank my first glass with shaky hands. I drank so much that night that I had a dream about peeing. I ended up wetting my bed for real. As a child I enjoyed wetting my bed when I was half-awake and half-asleep. Some of Farid's kids had jobs, while others were unemployed, stoned, and drunk.

"Farid?"

"Yes?"

"Have you read about writers thriving in solitude?"

"Yes."

"Do you believe it?"

He gave me a look like he didn't want to respond.

"Yes, but I promise that I won't bother you. I'll keep quiet unless you speak to me first. You won't feel my presence at all. I'll have my own solitude as well."

"It doesn't work that way. You'll be present even if you're an invisible ghost. If you want us to remain friends, then go and look for somewhere else to live."

"I'll feel a lethal loneliness if I live alone. That's what happened when they sent me to work in a village in the Rif Mountains. If it hadn't been for the psychiatrist who wrote the medical report that sent me back to Larache, I would've gone crazy."

"Farid?"

"Yes?"

"I'm helpless myself."

"Can I visit you?"

"Yes, you can. But there are times when I don't even want to know who's knocking on my door."

His visits would also make me uncomfortable. If I let him in, how was I going to convince him that I needed to be alone or go to sleep? That I wanted to take a break from talking and just meditate, write, read, dream, or listen to music with no one else around? I can come up with excuses to get rid of him when we're at a bar or coffee shop. But in my own home I'll have to make do with suppressing my anger, whether silently or by babbling. He's terribly, frighteningly sensitive. He just might bang his head against the wall if I hurt his feelings. He has numerous obsessions that he'll certainly take with him to the grave. Sometimes when he's at a bar or a coffee shop, he'll want to go where—as he puts it—the king goes alone. So, he'll finish off his glass, afraid that someone will try to put something in it to harm him. He does that even when he's with me.

"You don't trust me?" I asked.

"Who knows! Maybe you'll see an old acquaintance passing by the bar's window and go to catch up with them while I'm gone. Things that neither you nor I anticipate might happen. There are lots of crazy people everywhere who want to have fun, and haters who envy your lifestyle."

"But you don't have any enemies here, do you?"

"You never know what feelings people might be hiding from you, even if you don't know them."

He infected me with some of his contagious obsessions.

His assignment lasted only three weeks before they received a report from his psychiatrist and sent him back to Larache. He didn't visit me during that time. We didn't meet up. I saw him just once, walking toward the bus station. He was on the other side of the street. Did he notice me? I couldn't explain his refusal to see me, even at Bar Negresco. We both have our complexes, obsessions, and peculiarities. I don't regret anything that happened between us.

The last time he came up from Larache, he lamented to the bar's owner that I was traveling in Germany. When he was alone he'd always sit in front of the aquarium. He didn't care about anything other than his black fish, Nadia the Hippie—not the small turtle he called Sophie, not the other fish with their beautiful colors. He drank his beers until the very last drop.

The bar's regulars were accustomed to his involuntary move-
ments, so none of them made fun of him anymore. They were
more inclined to pity than to mockery. One day Farid saw something he didn't like. Nadia the Hippie had stopped moving her
fins. She was floating, not diving. She was motionless. Farid's
eyes popped out of his skull. He started twitching and shaking.

"That's not possible!" he yelled. "Nadia's sick. Nadia's
dying."

Everyone noticed his delirious shouting. "Something really
disturbing is happening with him today," they whispered.

Dr. Anwar, who was a pulmonologist, was sitting in his usual
corner by the entrance to the kitchen. He was reading his newspaper and sipping his fennel drink. He went over to Farid and
asked, "What's going on?"

Farid knew him well since he was one of the regulars. "Nadia's dying," he replied.

"Nadia?"

"Yes, my fish Nadia is dying. Look at her. She's floating and
has stopped moving. Save her!"

The doctor went behind the wooden bar and removed the
fish from its tank. He put her in a cup filled with water and proceeded to the kitchen, where he told Farid he'd give her CPR.
When he came back, she was still floating in the cup. He put her
back in the aquarium. She kept floating.

"I'm sorry. I did what I could. She's dead."

"Is it possible that the turtle hurt her? She looks ferocious.
Her quietness makes you doubt how peaceful she really is."

"I don't think so. The turtle is always in its usual corner or floating on its cork straw. My condolences. I too used to like that beautiful fish . . ."

"Nadia."

"Sorry, your poor fish Nadia."

Farid was in tears when he left. He never came back to Bar Negresco.

News about Death and the Deceased

People may say
That he has been resuscitated.
But his death has been prolonged,
Once by a rumor
And again by a joke.
His livelihood isn't enough
For him to die only once.
There is more than intrigue,
There is more than rancor
Making his death infinite.

Moncef's passion for news about death and the deceased started at an early age. Today he has become the city's roaming historian of death. He is the first, after the family, to find out that someone has passed away.

He'd scour French and Arabic newspapers for information and try very hard to sound out the Spanish ones. He'd pick up newspapers in cafés and bars, from customers whom he'd inform about those who had died that day or the day before and those who were dying. He didn't read the obituaries to learn something new about the deceased, unless the deceased had been a writer or an artist. The death of ordinary people barely received any coverage in newspapers. He was the one who knew everything about everyone in the city, including the immigrants, from the day they were born until the day they died. Any news he had about the death of someone—whether in Tangier or another city, near or far—was irrefutable. He'd color-code the death: red for murder, white for natural causes, and black for suffocation! He'd even be able to tell you if the person was good or bad. Every story included information about who the deceased was, was not, and could have been. Each one stemmed from reality or from an embellished version of reality. The way he'd tell the story and how much he'd say depended on how many drinks he was offered, how good his mood was, how much courtesy he was shown, and how close his relationship was with the person asking—whether that person was interested in the secrets of the deceased or in innocent information about the death. You'd basically hear as much as you wanted to know.

Moncef rarely respected the saying "speak well of the dead," especially when the dead had flaws. What he had to say about the deceased, good or bad, depended on the appetite and generosity of the listener. He'd start his story by saying either "poor so-and-so died" or "so-and-so, who died, was this and that."

He even had stories about the deaths of pets—dogs, cats, parrots, and birds—as well as of plants and inanimate objects. Every piece of news he ever told was a fact: "Antonia's dog died. She cried over him until she drunkenly pissed herself at Bar Le Grillon"; "There was a row of trees on the way to that private school. Three were cut down to make space for parents to park when they pick up their kids"; "The historic La Parade Bar will be demolished in order to construct a one-story building in its place."

No one could compete with Moncef in spreading news about death except death itself. His real job was as a broker; he'd arrange the rental or purchase of houses in the old city. He knew just as much about the old city's news and its houses—both solid and shaky—as he did about death and demolition. His greatest pleasure, though, was news of the dead, whether from his neighborhood or from others, near or far. His passion for death and news of the dead knew no bounds. Wherever people died, he'd know about it. He talked about them cheerfully. Sometimes he'd innocently start giggling, depending on how much fun the audience was and how much they liked his story about the latest death or his memories of other dead people from the city.

At funerals he'd walk with the people at the back. But as soon as the cortege approached the cemetery, he'd squeeze through the crowd so that he could be the first to enter—unless someone else got there before him. More than one child might be waiting for the cortege just outside the cemetery, or nobody might be waiting at all. El Aouni was the only kid who used to stand in his way. He had a small bearlike face and a big tummy that didn't match his age or short stature. Moncef was not jealous of El Aouni because he was a sweet and quiet boy and because he pitied his bulging belly. After the burial Moncef would fill his own belly with the bread and figs given to the mourners. He used to give his friends in the neighborhood the leftover food because the other mourners weren't hungry.

He didn't attend class regularly in high school, so he expelled himself before they could expel him. He stopped attending funerals once he started working. If the deceased was a neighbor or a close relative, he'd either fake an illness or travel to a northern city for several days to cover up his absence. He was interested in learning about the news of all those who had died, all those who were dying, and all those who were sick or disabled, but he was obsessed with spreading the news about the deaths of rich people and city officials. It was an opportunity for him to tell their life stories, from rags to riches or vice versa. He was never overwhelmed, sad, or happy when telling a story about a dead person, unless he sensed that the audience wanted him to feel that way.

When he first became interested in spreading news of death, he wasn't aware that what made the news important and intriguing for people was the amount of information he could provide and the stories he could concoct about the deceased. Moncef became an expert informant, with whom nobody could compete. He was the undisputed reference when it came to news of dead people in the city. The deceased people he would talk about in hushed tones were usually rich or powerful tyrants. He rarely spoke well of them, unless he wanted to butter up the person who was listening and who was eager to know the secrets of the deceased, whether true or false. He'd begin reporting on the dead before their death, at the onset of their chronic illness. He'd check to see if, for example, the retired professor was still walking twice a day in his neighborhood, as his doctor had recommended. If Moncef was not in a hurry, he'd even talk to the professor himself. The professor would take the opportunity to ask about the city's old bars and how they were changing. He continued to drink heavily until his illness took its toll. Moncef would see him from near or far more than once a week. Moncef did the same with Paul Bowles, who used to go on daily walks near the golf course, accompanied by his driver. He had just had surgery for sciatica. Whenever Moncef wanted to approach him to wish him a quick recovery, the driver's angry red eyes would scare him off.

I always saw Moncef in Barid Café. I had a routine with him. I'd stick the tip of my tongue out and twist it to the right. He'd smile and nod to indicate yes or no. If it was a no, I'd greet him from afar or maybe sit with him, reflecting on those who had recently passed away. But if it was a yes, I'd definitely sit with him. Between smiles and gentle laughter, he'd talk about the virtues or vices of the deceased. I'd go along with him, smiling and laughing in a bid to please him and get him to reveal every secret and scrap of information he possessed. When I'd ask him about someone I knew whose sudden death had shocked me, he'd tell me in a knowing tone how the person had been suffering from a chronic illness. He was always so certain of what he said, as though he had bet on a horse that was sure to win. "You know nothing," he seemed to be saying. "He was the favorite to pass away." If the deceased had been enjoying an extravagant lifestyle, he'd comment sarcastically and coldly, "He who enjoys his life should keep his eyes shut." But who could possibly be satisfied with what D'Annunzio said in his *Contemplation of Death*: "Once you've attained everything out of intelligence, contentment, or anger, you must let go of it all and disappear!"

Moncef moved near the cemetery and golf course. He never answered those who asked him about that choice, just as he never revealed why every death and funeral brought him so much joy.

Veronique

I fear for those who toy
With the word *love*
And those who believe in it.

I couldn't prove, with Veronique, that unexpected desire is the world's only gift. I couldn't examine the resistance inside me either, so I suppressed it. Perhaps I can only live freely with a woman in my imagination. I want her to be a mirage, an evasion, a lookout for what might happen between us and then fade into memory. It is the eternal ambition of poets. She couldn't understand why I disliked her knowing what I loved about her. Maybe neither of us intended what happened between us to happen. There are things that we both love, things that I love but she doesn't, and things that she loves but I don't. I couldn't care less if other people shared my passion for—or were just curious about—certain things, no matter how close those people were to me.

It is rare for a morning to pass without a stubborn fly buzzing around my table—whether at my house or here in the café—and landing on the lip of my cup or biting my hand, temple, or eyelid. I take a sweeping look at the street and the entrance to the post office. People of all kinds keep going in and out. I'd love to catch up with some of them, but others make me want to leave before they ruin the peace of my second cup of coffee. I'd even order a third just to lessen the burden of listening to their twisted, empty words. Sometimes, I'd get drinks simultaneously in the hope of casting some shade over their overpowering presence, which almost suffocates me. We'd end up fighting with the waiter—intentionally or not, depending on the savagery and aggression of our drunkenness—over a small misunderstanding with the check. We'd then refute each other or go our separate ways, making sure to remind each other to meet up again later that day or some other day.

As soon as I'd crush the first fly with my newspaper, the second and the third would arrive. One might seem stressed, the other relaxed, and another buzzing. I feel a childlike joy whenever they spoon each other; it makes crushing them easier, unexpected, and practically guaranteed from the first swat. They leave behind a disgusting stain, a mixture of red and white. When the weather gets colder and the café turns into a warm and welcoming place for flies, the crushing is endless, resulting in more of these disgusting splashes.

Today is a beautiful morning, one that I can start without flies buzzing in my ear or jumping ferociously around my cup. I'm just hoping not to see any of the people whose faces seem to invite spit and hold all the stupidity and futility of lives lived between narrow, disease-filled alleys. Whenever I look for similarities between me and others, I usually end up retreating back into myself.

Here comes the professor of the natural sciences, previously

dignified in his misery, now descending the boulevard. He's using both hands to grip the upturned collar of his coat. He seems
more hunchbacked in the winter, with his head tilted slightly
forward. Ever since he stopped speaking and started mumbling, his gait has almost slowed to a crawl. His clothes have
lost their original color, and his full head of hair now extends
down to his beard. It's a typical nest for a tolerant face, whose
features show only the joy or sadness that we imagine. Every
summer someone comes from overseas to see him. The man
cleans and dresses him, then disappears. Then the professor's
condition gets worse and worse until he reaches the state we
see him in today, waiting again for that mysterious person—a
relative, a friend, or just some random do-gooder—to show up.
At least according to a bartender at Bar Juana De Arco, where
the professor was a regular customer before he went to sleep
sane and woke up crazy, declaring his silence. This year the
professor seems to have grown hairier and dirtier. His savior is
late. Standing on the edge of the sidewalk, he pauses and snuffs
his tobacco. Dusting off his nose and hands, he steps down. The
professor usually paces up and down the boulevard until evening. I have no clue where he eats or sleeps. A passerby gives
him a coin. He doesn't even look at it. He doesn't beg, but he
never rejects people's charity either.

Carly goes up the boulevard, passes through the corniche,
then returns to his quarter in the Petit Socco. It was more than
thirty years ago that he too declared his silence and started having mumbled conversations with imaginary friends. He still
walks with swagger, making menacing gestures. Sometimes
the names of those he has accused of betrayal and wickedness

waft through the air like the ghosts of Zulaikha and Elmostafa. The professor intercepts him and places the coin in Carly's limp hand, as if entrusting him with something precious. Then the professor slowly continues on his way, but when Carly opens his hand to look at it, the coin falls. It starts rolling away before he can step on it. When he finally picks it up, a street kid just as miserable as Carly is standing in front of him, sniffing a rag soaked in kerosene. His eyes are clouded, and his mouth is open and dry. Smiling, Carly slips the coin into the child's limp hand. The kid goes back to where he came from, as if his only reason for appearing had been to catch the coin. He walks wearily.

Zohra showed up at the café and, cursing no one in particular, demanded a hundred dirhams—also from no one in particular. The waiter lit a cigarette for her and another for himself.

"They came and were disappointed," she said, staring at the ceiling.

She picked up the bucket that was full of her belongings, cursed a single individual, then left. Nuns take care of her more than once a year. Last time she showed up, she demanded four hundred riyals so that she could use the public restroom. Her hands and feet were as black as coal, and her misery was concentrated in her face. Sometimes she whirls and whirls like a dervish, never tiring of that dance. They once dressed her up in clothes that would've suited her better in her youth, a phase that many still remember. She started walking around us, middle-aged and almost naked. She definitely slept far from her young guardians' quarter, or maybe they themselves undressed her in a crazy dance. Everything is permissible in their brotherly group. It was as though she were their mother, and they

didn't know where else to turn. At night she'd provide a loving
embrace for those sniffers of kerosene-soaked rags. One morning she surprised us all with a face of full makeup. Maybe her
guardians had wanted to beautify her wrinkly face and pursed
lips, which look more like a scar than a mouth, as if someone
had carved a toothless hole with a razor blade. Woe to any busy-
body who tried to approach her when she was surrounded by
her kids. They'd rip him apart with their clawed hands. He'd
be lucky if they didn't use sharp tools. Passersby would have
to go another way or keep their heads down. A simple greeting would suffice; anything more risked irking them or rousing
their concern.

Veronique enters, and my eyes go straight to her cleavage,
which can be either a joyful or a disturbing sight. In the morning we only greet each other with glances and smiles. Her
breakfast consists of unsweetened black tea. I had pointed out
that she was fatter and shared my distaste for the way her tight
pants clung to her butt. All she wore now were long skirts so as
to appeal to me. It was a form of possession and subjugation.
I regretted my remark. Our intermittent chat might begin after
I've had my third or fourth glass and she's had her second or
third beer and we've smoked some cigarettes or maybe taken
some snuff to sneeze and sober back up. That only happens
when some jerk is snorting it and lets us have some. Sometimes
I have no idea how to stop her from drinking, while at other
times I fail to convince her to join me in drowning my sorrows
and disappointments. She may stubbornly resist, or she may
drink one glass after another. At that point I stop insisting that
she drink with me so that the other customers don't start to pity

her and ridicule me. I have no idea how to rid myself of my barbaric tyranny.

There's a lively debate taking place between Emile Habibi and Elias Khoury at Hanan al-Shaykh's house. When I looked at the bottle between us, I realized that it was empty. I had only drunk two glasses. Veronique was mesmerized by the men, staring as though she were hanging on every word of their analysis of the war between the Arabs and Jews over Palestine—the war that had revealed the weakness and savagery of the Arabs through Black September. But she only knew the few words of Moroccan Darija that she had learned from prostitutes in the popular bars of Tangier she so admires and adores. I didn't have the necessary qualifications to participate in their critical discussion. They didn't seem to care; my presence was insignificant. Hanan al-Shaykh appeared, as if on a magic carpet, then put another bottle in front of us and withdrew, wishing us good health.

"Veronique," I said as she filled our glasses, "we're not going to spend the night here."

She stared at me blankly, then focused her wooden gaze on Emile and Elias.

"You know that I have no idea how to transfer on the Underground," I continued.

It was my first time visiting London. One of the cultural associations had brought me there. Veronique's statue-like gaze was fixed on Emile Habibi and Elias Khoury, who were more relaxed after a few glasses of whiskey. Their frenzied discussion had wound down and now they were talking as if recollecting on Palestine and Lebanon before and after the war.

"I promise we'll arrive safely," she said.

I started drinking from the bottle to make sure that her glass would not be refilled as quickly as she was emptying it. I can't remember how we left or how we changed lines on the Underground. The Victoria, where we were staying, seemed far away. Which of us supported the other until we arrived? Neither of us can remember or even pretend to remember. Maybe we guided each other. The bite of the street woke me up a little, so I ordered a glass of whiskey and she ordered a beer. Elias Khoury was staying at the same hotel. He stood up in front of our table and said, "In an interview with *Paradise Magazine* you said that I was impotent. I'm a real man—if you only knew!"

"That was nothing . . ."

I offered to buy him a drink to lighten his mood, but he declined. He said that he was going to sleep. I noticed him wandering around the bar, then he left.

"What were you two talking about?" Veronique asked.

"Just something silly that happened years ago at the Solazur Hotel. His friend, the poet Mahmoud Darwish, was teasing me about his virility, which he used to boast about wherever he went, like some playboy. Elias was egging him on. I was their victim that morning. I went to wake them up because Darwish, along with two other poets, was supposed to read his poetry that evening in Rabat. While he was putting on his perfume, he asked if I owned a villa in Jbel Kbir. I told him that I did not. He then said that I didn't know how to get rich even though I was Jean Genet and Tennessee Williams's bitch, or something like that. I said that he was smarter and more seductive than me, so we should just split the prize if he wanted me to show

him where he could be a real man. I nearly drank an entire bottle of whiskey that ill-fated morning, one glass after another,
just to control my temper. But they stopped me. They can't get
hard—true or false, that's what I said about them to a journalist
in Paris."

Veronique laughed. "The story of the goat and the doe—a
Bedouin joke," she said. "He could have had a drink with us.
He looked sad to me."

"True. He was breastfed on sadness and couldn't, or just
didn't want to, be weaned off it."

I don't know how to stop Veronique from loving cats so
much. Two young musicians invited us to a party at somebody's
house in La Rochelle. Her eyes got redder and redder, filling
with tears, and her nose kept running, but she wouldn't stop
petting, holding, and kissing the big fat cat. She pet it again and
again until I got disgusted. I pictured her naked, sticky everywhere I touched her. I threatened to ditch the party, which she
was really enjoying, if she didn't leave the old cat alone—its fur
now covering her sweater. She stopped petting it but kept wink-
ing at it and luring it over with her smiles every time I looked
away. Eventually I'd had enough of her childish games. Our
lovely host, however, looked very pleased with the stupidity
of his cat. When he saw Veronique gently petting it, he told us
that his little sister did the same. He didn't get jealous, not even
once, of Veronique. The damn cat didn't miss its owner, didn't
long for him to hug and pet it as much as it wanted. The owner
was happy to extol the merits of his cat, who was oh-so-wise
and one of a kind. How I wished he would tempt his cat with
pets and coos, but they seemed to have made a pact: whenever

people came and went, they'd stay sweetly apart from each other. Damn them!

When it comes to what I love that she represses, and what she loves that I avoid, Veronique is the master of her feelings. Our passions are as open as we want them to be, the way it was with my beloved Fati too.

We were staying with Julie and Mohamed. I expressed my obsessive desire to visit three cemeteries: Père Lachaise, Montparnasse, and Montmartre. I have this urgent and persistent desire to visit the villages and cities of the dead in any country I visit, even if I don't know anyone buried there. Julie begged her son Bertrand to drive us to those kingdoms of the dead. He insisted that I sit next to him—to enjoy more of the scenery, he told me. He drove carefully, explaining the origins of the streets to me. He knew their entire history, as if he were reading straight from both old and new maps. I was demonstrating my interest, while Mohamed and Veronique stayed silent, whispered, or shared jokes. Bertrand seemed just as enthusiastic as his mother, who works like a beaver.

"It really is the city of the dead," I said to Mohamed after we had walked along one of the numbered pathways. "I've never seen anything more beautiful. Some cemeteries are full of garbage."

"It's a cosmic cemetery. Here you'll find most of the people you've read about, from every nationality."

Here and there we received Tower of Babel vibes. Bertrand and Veronique stopped in front of Joseph Ginsburg's family plot. His son's grave was covered in flowers, some planted,

others potted, and still others wrapped in plastic; pictures of
him and his fans; his favorite ceramic ashtray, which looked
like a shell or maybe an ear; handwritten cards; a coin; a pillow
embroidered with flowers; and a sad-looking plush dog, which
was lying on an embossed piece of marble:

> *To you Serge*
> From your friends
> *OF HOPE*

They had forgotten to bring him a five-hundred-franc banknote,
which he used to use to roll the cigarettes he'd smoke in front
of his television audience. A spaceship that became a symbol
for a blue trip.

I had never heard of him before I met Veronique. She bought
a CD of his songs. Even if his lyrics were clever, I wasn't thrilled
by his singing. She got slightly annoyed and sighed. Maybe it
was because, unlike her, I wasn't nineteen years old. But when
she gave me a present of Satie's songs and I became even more
obsessed with him than she was, she forgave me for not liking
her idol, Ginsburg, so much. She gets along well with Bertrand
and Julie but not so well with Mohamed. We both keep sticking
to the vague desire with which we protect ourselves.

Mohamed and I stopped in front of the graves of Colette and
her daughter. Two unfaded bouquets. I thought about how there
were still some people who remembered *Gigi* and *The Vagabond*. I also thought about how it was probably only women
who had brought all the bouquets and pots there.

The epitaph on the tomb of Alexandre Dumas fils was artisti-
cally inscribed. A rusty nail was stuck in the nose of the marble
statue above his grave.

"What a strange piece of vandalism." I sighed.

I envisioned a crazy man at night, waving his hammer here
and placing a flower there, kissing one grave and peeing on
another—affectionate, then cruel, by turns. He seems to have
bewildered all the people who might've tried to put an end to
his delusions. Dormant desires possess people, and the possessed enforce the sovereignty of the night—their night. The
possessed are like owls, who wait patiently for their prey to
finish devouring its own so that they can easily feast on both.

"A lot of things happen here at night," Mohamed told me,
bringing me back from my reveries. "Sadists jump on top of
the walls. They may even burn trees. There is an extraordinary
number of trees in Père Lachaise—around twelve thousand,
they say. The day brings its own madmen as well. The grave of
the journalist Victor Noir (1848–70) is over there. The bronze
statue above it by the artist Dalou is considered a masterpiece. It
shows his penis. Some women touch and kiss it. Maybe they're
barren and think that, by touching, kissing, or even sucking it,
they'll get pregnant. They'd probably even swallow it if they
could. Or maybe it's a way of satisfying their fantasies or of
getting married before they reach menopause. The shy ones just
whisper repeatedly, 'Victor, dear Victor.' They're terrible. But
they're nothing compared to Sergeant Bertrand. In the middle
of the nineteenth century, he'd sleep with women's corpses,
then disembowel them and chop them up. Nothing quite so

gruesome has happened in Père Lachaise or other cemeteries since."

Modest flowers were sprouting from a small iron pot. Beside it was an empty bottle, waiting for someone to fill it with water again—a loyal gesture, perhaps, from a lover of both Alexandre Dumas fils and the heroine of *The Lady of the Camellias*. Marguerite Gautier's desire to buy the flowers she so adored was, perhaps, even more intense than her need to purchase her medication. She was a martyr to quicksilver love, fatal sickness, and a bankruptcy that led to a public auction to pay back her debts.

The black marble of a beautiful two-level tomb caught my attention. The names of Mohamed and Christine were inscribed on it. Just a few steps away, another grave was inscribed in Hebrew.

"Don't be surprised. Anyone who can afford to be buried here can be buried here, assuming they can find an open plot."

Gérard de Nerval's grave was the luckiest when it came to expensive flower bouquets. I wonder if he thought about the woman who looked like his mother before he hanged himself. He wrote, "I never saw my mother. All I know is that she resembled an engraving of the time, which was called *Modesty*. It represented a beautiful young woman: her eyes were shy, her nose was slim, and her small mouth was drawn with extreme precision."

His father had served as a medic in the Grande Armée during the era of Napoleon's victories. His mother had died of a fever while accompanying his father across a bridge that was piled high with corpses on their way to hell. His father wore the sign of mourning for the rest of his life. Gérard kept looking for the one in the multiple, for the face of his mother in the faces of all the women he never tired of inventing. Women of dreams, delusions, and magical mysteries. A specter of a face swinging between the void and death, where the dream is the master of reality and legend overshadows history. It is the same bitter pain that Jean Genet suffered over his unknown mother and his lover Abdallah, for whose face he kept searching in an endless number of faces. He felt guilty for encouraging Abdallah to elevate his art, because his inability to reach those heights may have led him to his death.

Mohamed drew my attention to the grave of Oscar Wilde, the crazy aphorist, the angelic, the winged, the eunuch. "As you can see," he said, "anything can happen here."

For his mourners
will be outcast men
And outcasts
always mourn

Balzac's statuesque grave was overflowing with all the flowers that he described in his books. Alfred de Musset's and Rossini's graves were neglected. None of the leafy green shadows that Musset had wished for were covering his grave.

The garden of Baudelaire's grave formed its own kingdom. Its mummified appearance did not detract from its grace. It was—of course it was—graceful and more. It had all the space he adored in his protective solitude. No one was crowding him. There was a grave there, and another over there. His stepfather was buried—against Baudelaire's will—not too far away, as if the General's medals would protect him. The leaves were a mix of greens and new yellows. The soil that was scattered around his grave could have been from Mars or Venus. It seemed to me that all this was a good match for his mood. He had renounced his homeland to find his homeland. Maybe he thought that beauty had no homeland. He didn't gamble with his life to gain stupid friends.

> Then what do you love, extraordinary
>   stranger?
> I love the clouds, the clouds that pass up there,
> Up there the wonderful clouds!

You are luckier than the poet who resembles the albatross:

> The Poet is like the prince of the clouds,
> Who haunts the tempest and mocks the archer;
> Exiled on the earth in the midst of derision,
> His giant wings keep him from walking.

Bertrand and Veronique are far behind us. They are a few years apart in age. It's difficult for her to establish a relationship with him. His love for his girlfriend, Asmahan, is unshakable. Their shadows form another, thicker shadow, impenetrable by any human light or dust. The two of them are the only human models in all love's legendary paintings. Their selves belong to them alone; no human feeling can penetrate them. Alone in the world, they wander through forests and ride fierce animals that they have tamed. Veronique might have managed to form a bond with their big cat, as she did with the one owned by our host in La Rochelle. But their cat is less friendly. She might have had to use her devilry to befriend it. I know her and I know the cat. It's allergic to the caresses of some people. I once saw it sneeze and clean itself after being touched by Tina, Asmahan's friend. If someone the cat doesn't like tries to pet it more than once, it might disappear or run off to surveil from a distance. It doesn't vamp the way cats usually do. I thought it had a lot of pride and swagger for a cat. Veronique begged me—unsuccessfully—to adopt a stray. It never left my neighborhood. One day before leaving Tangier, she named it Cali. She was talking to, petting, and feeding it, and eventually I got tired of waiting for her. She'd catch up with me at the café.

"Take it with you to Brussels. Take it!" I said. "I'm sure your grandmother would take care of it the way she takes care of the wild squirrels in her garden."

"She doesn't like cats, unfortunately."

"I don't like the cat either. I admire its pride but only from afar."

I found out later from Mohamed that Bertrand had driven us unwillingly. To him I seemed like an idiot. He told his mother that he was surprised by my obsessive interest in the three cemeteries. She chided him for questioning my weird obsession. She might have been thinking, in her usual kind way, about how people hope when they're alive that others will visit them when they're dead.

When I visited Paris for the second time, Bertrand gave me a leather flask for alcoholics. It was ready to be filled with my favorite drinks so that I could get through the cold Parisian February. He also happily offered to take me to Picpus Cemetery, where the beheaded—noble and commoner alike—slumber so that the republic can celebrate its bloody glory, confirming the saying that "revolution preys on its children." And why not? At the end of the day, we are all beheaded. Then he asked me if I wanted to visit the Montmartre and Montparnasse cemeteries again. Was it out of regret? to please his mother, the devoted host? or out of a sudden desire he hadn't discovered until now?

Mohamed, Veronique, and I walked along Rue Mouffetard. Bertrand went to see his girlfriend Asmahan, who was waiting for him at his mother's house.

"Verlaine used to drag his cane here," Mohamed said. "It would carry his weight, then turn into a stick for other things, like beating up his publisher who ripped him off over his publications rights. He'd find a bouquet of his favorite flowers, sent by an anonymous fan, on his table at Café Procope."

A wild rabbit as large as a lamb was hanging. We asked them to prepare it for our return. Everything was cut into pieces, except for the blood that was gathered under its plastic-wrapped head. I told them they could do whatever they wanted with the blood; such offal made me sick. I suggested that it be cooked with dried prunes and served with hard-boiled eggs. Mohamed agreed with me, and Veronique didn't have a better idea. One of her better qualities is that she likes everything I cook. Maybe it was a way for her to discover new things? If I had been in Tangier, either by myself or with her, I would've cooked it with fennel. Julie likes my cooking too. She admits that she's not a very good cook herself. Her work as a translator and writer doesn't give her much time to flirt and dally with cooking. One of my habits is to bring over spices from Tangier, even though they're all available here. Even ras el hanout. The spices may look alike and share the same name, but they taste different. Spices from Tangier are laced with nostalgia. At least that's what Mohamed says every time someone hassles him about why he hasn't visited his homeland in over twenty years.

Le Mayflower is famous for its excellent cheeses and wines. At the bar I told Mohamed that I could still smell a hint of Hemingway, Fitzgerald, and probably even Faulkner. He said I was not wrong. I thought about Dean's Bar.

"Someone's looking through the peephole," Veronique said as we were about to fall asleep.

"So what? If there's a peephole, someone might as well look through it."

She sighed as usual.

I thought it might've been an illusion that occurs before falling sleep, or it might've been true. Her vision is sharp. I got up, closed the door, and blocked it with a chair.

"Look!" she said the next morning. "The chair's been moved from its place."

That could be true, or she could be faking it. I know all about her childish tricks. She loves disputes and thinks that it's all right to foment them herself. She is wicked as well, though in a nice way.

"The eye of the night is enchanted by whispers, kisses, embraces, and erotic pulses. The eye of the night is behind every single door. Remember the hotel's owner in Brussels? She eavesdropped on our bed's rhythm. 'Is she your daughter?' the dreadful woman had asked before filling out our reservation forms. She didn't approve of you being my lover. Do you remember? It's obvious that she didn't get fucked enough, that human chicken."

Since that interaction with the hotel's owner, we've decided to make her my daughter and me her father. Pretending to be a dad and his daughter was more about having fun than about hiding the fact that we were dating.

Her mom was taking a nap. I couldn't tell whether she was asleep or just relaxed. I'm always wary of mothers' sleep. I didn't ask Veronique about the depth of her mom's naps. Would I have been able to believe what she said anyway? She's one to toss a lit firecracker into your hand and let you handle it. We were fondling each other in the living room, while Mozart, the canary, was singing and jumping between two bars of his cage.

"Let's do it here!" she said excitedly "We'll do it here."

"Your mom's asleep," I replied, "or she might even be awake."

"I don't care. We'll do it here. Why does it matter that she's there?"

"The balcony might be better."

Her face lit up, and she rushed over there, practically chanting "hallelujah, hallelujah." I thought about her mother waking up. Mothers' hunches and instincts are always strong. We had a hard time getting onto the balcony through the bathroom window. I didn't know what to do about my horniness. A touch below, a touch above, a touch everywhere. Touching multiplied, mouth to mouth and hand stroking hair.

"Maybe we can do it outside the apartment in the stairwell," I suggested.

Her face lit up even more. We closed the door quietly. We didn't want to risk the neighbors hearing us if we lay down in the hallway, so we enjoyed each other madly while standing. We were playing a role that no one could see. We could be whatever we wanted to be, even if that meant being a bit less crazy. A day might come when we can't come here. I was more or less dismissive of Veronique's erotic whims. She said that we would do it there. I said no, impossible. We were of two minds about the where of the matter, but that didn't bother us. I realized that she was defying and provoking her mother, even when she wasn't there. Maybe she really wanted her mother to walk in while one of us was on top of the other. We were gasping for air, even though we did less than half of what our madness desired. We went back to the room. I lay down on the floor, and she lay down on the bed. I belonged to myself, and she to herself. Neither of us questioned the other's silence. Our silence was the conversation. We looked at each other, then I fell asleep. I didn't realize what she had done to the roof.

Her mom woke up before us. She was walking on the balcony, looking out at the sea and Charf Hill. She touched a plant with the back of her hand, then smelled a red rose. "You own more than a balcony," she said as she hummed to herself. "It's a floating garden."

She had come to see how her daughter was living in Tangier. She was told that Veronique was living with a dreadful writer, addicted to alcohol, drugs, and everything bad. What a shame for a daughter from an illustrious and respected family! How could she have ended up like this? But her mother saw none of what she heard. We booked her a room at Hôtel El Djenina.

I introduced to her a Moroccan painter who was unsuccessful in both her artistic and married life, hoping that the painter might entertain her. "What's your daughter doing with that old alcoholic writer?" she asked. "He'll ruin her. Take her with you. That's my advice." That's what Veronique told me after hearing about it from her mother. The painter who betrayed our friendship spends her time sucking on limp, shriveled oil dicks from the Gulf. When she's taken from behind, she complains that it's smaller than what she's used to. But from the front, she moans in satisfaction.

Veronique's mother invited me, her daughter, and the cocksucking painter for lunch at El Minzah Hotel. At my apartment I cooked for both mother and daughter. Her mother was fascinated by the city's delights and wanted to stay—at least until her daughter went back with her. She was nearly sixty years old but didn't look her age. I really liked her youthfulness. Her face lit up as she said goodbye to us at the airport. Maybe she'll tell her husband and mother that, contrary to what she'd been told, there was nothing suspicious about her daughter's relationship with the old writer. The mother was herself keeping busy by writing romantic stories in which she was the protagonist. She'll probably be the only person to ever read them. Her way of thinking was not compatible with the art of writing. She was writing, but the writing was waiting for style.

"Your mom's patience with you," I told Veronique, "is more generous than your mockery of her."

"I'm just teasing," she replied. "I'm allowed to joke with my mom."

The truth is that Veronique loved her mom in her own way. I

knew that she wanted to stay until she spent all the money that she had received from her generous mother and that she had saved from her two years working at a café in Brussels. But I decided to put an end to our adventure.

"Go back to your mom and to your studies, Veronique," I told her. "Go back to yourself or to whatever is far away from me. I don't belong to anyone but myself."

And so it was. She went back to whatever it was that she wanted to go back to. We stopped seeing each other, calling each other, or even writing to each other. I don't know whether she's alive or dead.

"Veronique?"

"Yes?"

"Shall we go home for lunch?"

"Can't we have another drink at the Alhambra?"

"Yes, we can."

We usually stopped at the Alhambra on our way home. She loved to spend time chatting with some of the prostitutes there.

My Face through the Seasons

We didn't have a mirror at home
Because none of us wanted to see our faces in it.

In Tangier, my city of wonders, I get hit by a wave of depression whenever I struggle against myself for no good reason. In the morning I get depressed when I can't remember a beautiful dream with which to start my day. I cling to dreams, because they are like Ariadne's thread in the city's labyrinth; they protect me from being soaked by the torrential rains of despair. I had a friend who believed that anybody who didn't know how to dream should come to Tangier. That's the way it was. That same friend, however, turned into an unbeliever, and so the city dragged him into its own particular hell. If it's the biggest dreamers who fashion the world, then I've let my dream fashion its own world.

When I forget the words, the images that they form still remain.

I'm disgusted when I discover that someone I considered a friend is just an opportunist. I embalm him, placing him in one of the corners of my memory's cemetery, as a reminder of a part of my life.

I have discovered that a little excitement helps reanimate my heart, and a good deal of anger helps paralyze my body and scramble my thoughts. When I'm angry, my memory is useless.

My childhood is the darkest cloud in my life. No one ever rewarded me. I was just a child to be slapped. There wasn't ever a single smile. I was living a life in which I could change nothing, because grown-ups were in control of everything. How will I ever be able to confront what I went through as a child? My thoughts were neither fearful nor brave, because I simply could not stop what was happening. I came to realize that a bitter life awaited me, so I let it happen. In order to reward myself until that time came, I created my own childhood wonders. And if today I feel proud of being a witness to my own childhood and to the childhoods of others like me, it is because, in most of my writing, I do my best to unveil their darker moments. Everyone's life has its clouds—some of them clear, others still hazy. Every childhood is like that. The village where I grew up has left no trace in my memory. It is just a distorted screen upon which pictures are projected—of myself, of others, and of misshapen forms. That childhood was destroyed by migration. I do not believe people who claim to remember their entire childhood. They may have some vague sense of it, but it is only a glimmer of light in a very dark sky. It's impossible to know to what extent authors' childhoods influence their writing. They write about childhood from the perspective of mature adults. They circle around it because every childhood is hostage to its adulthood. The "childness" of childhood can be understood only by the child.

When the clouds of my life collide, my sleepy state of waiting is roused. I believe in leading a life of emergencies. The clouds of my life urge me to grab whatever slips away from it. My life is like a piece of flint: once it ignites, it becomes a spark, then a flame, and then light.

I love mystery, quarrels, mirages, echoes, buds, the phoenix, the magic of ripples, and temptation. I am who I am, and I long for creation's root to burst into bloom.

Whenever distress invades my life, I tap my reservoir of experiences to fight back. For my personal fortress, I have constructed a secret crypt; for my pyramid, its own locked exit; and for my tower, its pathfinder telescope.

I am an Aries. I live between night and day. The wolf has the right to devour me, but I have the right to outsmart him and fight back.

My symbol will last, but my life won't.

In our present we are always hard on the past. It's like a grandmother we accuse of having dementia, forgetting that she was the one who shaped our imagination with her storytelling. If the past takes the form of a grandmother—the fountain of language—then the present is nothing but her grandson.

My coldness is not a seed that was born with me and then grew until it had deep, far-reaching roots. Whatever I have gained from my past experiences and traumas—seedlings that were planted here and there in the realm of my life—I have uprooted from its arboretum. My coldness is only a fleeting depression.

I was sitting alone at El Dorado when Larbi El Yacoubi passed by to remind me of his upcoming birthday. While waiting for his birthday, we had some champagne to celebrate mine. That's how

I managed to overcome the worrisome aspects of turning sixty-four—with a moment of friendship.

Spring

Books and writing are the two sources that have never dried up since bursting into my life. They suppress my usual sense of time, creating a new sense of time that deepens creativity. They guide both my dreams and my apprehensions. They free me from narrow vision and lead me toward a broader perspective, an internal exile.

A glance can only capture the entirety of space when it's in our dreams. The ultimate goal is to realize our own dreams before realizing the dreams of others.

The fountain of dreams never dries up if it reaches Don Quixote's level of madness. He moves from one dream to another, one conquest to another, until he grows feeble. Victory does not matter to those obsessed with eternity. What would Don Quixote do with his life if he ever lost his madness? We might start with a dream and end up with madness. Don Quixote lived a fool and died a sage, as is written on his grave. . . . Who can be like him?

Adventure is the only fountain from which I filch fleeting happiness.

I picked up my first win when I dedicated myself to reading and writing and rid myself of the curse of my government job, with its boasting bosses and ass-kissing employees hoping for a promotion. Now I can get drunk on my own nectar. I have always preferred to be alone, winning or losing, in my work. I have let creativity well up from existence and nothingness, from fullness and emptiness, from futility and counteraction to the higher cause.

The creative person is someone who instills in me the seed-ling of effusion and transcendence, someone who can plant words and use them to shape visions and imaginations. I do not believe in a hope that is devoid of my own ambitions and hard work. Such a hope engenders procrastination and distraction. Only a child has the right to hope. Indeed, children can't change a thing. If they do, then it was a miracle or coincidence.

Nature tugs at my heartstrings when I pluck its guitar and imitate it. I am inside its heart, and it is inside mine. The nature created by our imagination is more beautiful than nature itself. When I am far away from it, I am deeply intoxicated by its winds and sounds. Nature is what shapes our characters. It is from nature that we derive the things that encourage us when we are sad. It is our refuge when we fall out of harmony with human nature.

The most beautiful flower in my life is wild. Its scent disap-pears when one approaches it; it withers when one sows it. It grows and gives off scent only when it is in its own volcanic clay. Its name is carved in its arboretum, and it vanishes when it goes back to its ashy eternity. Every time it is resurrected, it adopts a different color, like a chameleon. It uses its poisonous nectar to protect its virginity so that no one can pick it without the antidote on hand. Call it the Goddess of Flowers, if you like, for it does not have a name.

I'll donate the rest of my life to anyone who can use it to

shed light in the tunnel of people's thoughts. I don't care so much about people's identities as about their effectiveness. I realize that my life's bouquet will be very thorny. I should hand it only to someone with a calloused hand. Maybe I'll leave it to whoever wants it.

The word *success* reminds me of a theatrical smile or a sneaky business deal. I do not like to cram myself into an auction, bidding for success, because it violates my ambition.

Summer

It was unbearably hot, waiting for the unknown. Many things happened but not what we wanted. I lost only as much as I won. I didn't go all in. There are paradises I've heard about. I had been eager to see them, but I changed my mind. Today I do not crave "a garden, high and fertile: heavy rain falls on it but makes it yield a double increase of harvest" (Quran 2:265). Yearning robs me of life's pleasures.

Too much honesty is a folly that only leads to recklessness. I might be scorched by a madness that unleashes joy and awakens the delights of beauty.

An image only excites me when it manages to inspire the creation of the image dwindling inside it.

Absolute frankness is a death penalty to every possibility of agreement.

When I confess what I know about people and things, I create an enemy that might, unbeknownst to me, take revenge on me, even in my own imagination.

Honesty is not always the ultimate truth. What keeps me tied to reality is the joyful idea that I create about it and the temptations with which it challenges me.

The thing that I relish about the throng of life is the extent to which its stench disperses. I do not expect someone to make me happy. I'm the one who has to make myself—in all my moods—happy.

I never touch a wild beauty. I only toy with what is hidden. Ostentation is allowable for the impotent, but as the traditional tale has it, there's no buttermilk for every Dakhtanūs in summer.

The cold breeze that refreshes me is the one that takes me by surprise, like summer rain.

A little bit of hatred gets the blood flowing, stretches the arteries, and gets the heart pumping again. A lot of hatred, however, blows everything apart. The same applies to paranoia: a little bit might inspire creativity, but a lot results only in delusion and schizophrenia.

If I have an important meeting with someone I hate, I insult him in the bathroom of my own home. That way, when I actually meet him, I don't feel the need to insult him again—out loud or in secret.

I hate those who stop me from writing. I don't know how to make peace with them other than through writing, which always wins against prohibition.

I feel how sweet life is when I wake up and bestow my morning glances from my balcony, like an eagle soaring ever higher; when I can discern everything in sight, everything I retrieved from my happy imagination, and everything I dreamed; when I can recall enjoying the first sip from a vintage wine; when what

I listen to reminds me of a woman I used to love and she knocks on my door; when my desire to dream in solitude defeats human temptation. Whenever I have all or part of this at my disposal, I feel the sweetness of life, as the clawing cats inside my head calm down and submit.

I'm served an iced drink by my mother, a female friend, or the woman I just met. I'm cautious about what lovers serve me, even if it comes from their mouths. I'm even careful around my own sisters.

I do not necessarily drink my iced drink during a heat wave. I savor it in sips, not gulps. The wild grapes may come from a fox, a bear, a snake, or a colocynth.

Autumn

A person sheds his leaves when he dries up; new ones may grow back if his roots run deep and his water table is not depleted. Leaves do not change color, fade, or fall in the same way. Every leaf falls at a different stage—maybe even breaking off before it matures—and for a different reason. It is well known that everything that grows and has leaves is fated to decay.

I didn't acknowledge my autumn years until I felt completely incapable of doing things that I could easily do before. Death may well catch us before we enter the autumn of life. No one can guarantee the fruits of paradise.

Humans are either wise or senile, the harvester or the harvested, in their autumn years.

Sweet things taste bitter to me, and bitter things sweet.

I am no longer tempted by feasts unless they are plain and simple. I no longer sigh over what I once had and let slip, whether willingly or not. I remember everything, and I don't. I do not cling to a brittle branch even if it's dripping with honey. I face life's pallor by mixing yellow, blue, and white until I arrive at my color. I was never overcome by a life of austerity. I remain in touch with life, but I do not confront its stormy waves. When I set sail at the right time, I usually reach my destination.

There is no such thing as a victorious or a defeated hero. All heroism involves servitude. I am my own servant. To me, ambition is a kind of achievement and a by-product of stupidity.

Like leaves, dreams are not alike in the way they fall. Some dreams are strong; others are weak, transparent, foggy, joyful, or scary. We do not choose our dreams, and yet they are closely connected with our consciousness and subconsciousness. Many of our dreams reveal secrets of a past or future life. Our dreams are our fate, whether we accept or reject their magic. Dreams can often illuminate the shadows of our life and inspire us to reach our goals. When I wake, I seek refuge in daydreams, though they're not as powerful as real dreams, which hold the keys to our secret life. My face holds my magical dreams.

I don't care how many leaves fall from my autumn tree. It has already offered its color, fruit, taste, and nectar. Everything happened, whether I wanted it to or not. All I can recall of my sorrows are the things that soften their roughness and urge me to remember their more pleasant facets. We are not defined by how we end or how we begin; things may end the way they begin or begin the way they end. We are how we become.

About the Author and Translator

Mohamed Choukri (1935–2003) was a key figure in twentieth-century Arabic literature. Born in Morocco, he did not learn to read or write until he was in his twenties. *For Bread Alone*, the controversial English translation of Choukri's autobiographical work *al-Khubz al-ḥāfī*, was called "a true document of human desperation, shattering in its impact" by Tennessee Williams. Long censored by the Moroccan government for its taboo depictions of human suffering, poverty, prostitution, and homosexuality, among other things, Choukri's text nevertheless managed to circulate throughout the Arabic-speaking world, inspiring artists and authors alike. Choukri's oeuvre includes many works, such as the two collections of his short stories collected in *Tales in Tangier*. His autobiographical trilogy comprises *For Bread Alone*, *Streetwise*, and *Faces*. Choukri is also the author of three literary portraits, *Jean Genet in Tangier*, *Tennessee Williams in Tangier*, and *Paul Bowles in Tangier*; a play, *Zoco Chico*; and a book of essays.

Jonas Elbousty holds a PhD from Columbia University. He is a writer, a literary translator, and an academic. He teaches in the Department of Near Eastern Languages and Civilizations at Yale, where he was the director of undergraduate studies for seven years. He is currently the director of undergraduate studies at the Council on Middle East Studies at the Yale MacMillan Center. He is the author or coauthor of eight books, and his work has appeared in *ArabLit*, *ArabLit Quarterly*, *Asheville Poetry Review*, *Banipal*, *Michigan Quarterly Review*, *Prospectus*, *Sekka*, *Comparative Literature*, the *International Journal of Middle East Studies*, the *Journal of New Jersey Poets*, and the *Journal of North African Studies*, among other publications. His translation *The Screams of War* is forthcoming from Seagull Books.